THE Sweetheart QUEST

SWEETHEART ESCAPES BOOK 4

JACY BRAEGAN

Copyright © 2023 Jacy Braegan

All rights reserved.

No part of this book may be reproduced in any form or by an electronic or mechanical means, including information storage and retrieval systems, without written permission from the author, except for the use of brief quotations in a book review.

Cover Art & Formatting by Whimsical Reverie Design LLC (http://whimsicalreverie.design)

Table of Contents

Chapter 1: Trevor 1

Chapter 2: Rhodes 8

Chapter 3: Trevor 16

Chapter 4: Rhodes 21

Chapter 5: Trevor 27

Chapter 6: Rhodes 34

Chapter 7: Trevor 40

Chapter 8: Rhodes 47

Chapter 9: Trevor 52

Chapter 10: Rhodes 57

Chapter 11: Trevor 62

Chapter 12: Rhodes 66

Chapter 13: Trevor 70

Chapter 14: Rhodes 75

Chapter 15: Trevor 81

Chapter 16: Rhodes 86

Chapter 17: Trevor 92

Chapter 18: Rhodes 98

Chapter 19: Trevor................................102

Chapter 20: Rhodes 107

Chapter 21: Trevor................................ 112

Chapter 22: Rhodes................................ 117

Chapter 23: Trevor................................122

Chapter 24: Rhodes 127

Chapter 25: Trevor................................132

Chapter 26: Rhodes................................135

Chapter 27: Trevor................................139

Chapter 28: Rhodes................................145

Chapter 29: Trevor................................149

Chapter 30: Rhodes 155

Chapter 31: Trevor................................ 161

Epilogue: Trevor 165

Synopsis

Finding out my blind date is one of my gamer friends? Awesome. Finding out he's also my boss? Kill me now.

Trevor

When my best friend suggested a blind auction to aid in my shy self losing my v-card, I thought he was insane. If a hook up weirds me out, why would a blind date be different? Especially one no one I know can vouch for. While I'd rather have it be the guild mate I flirt with in-game, somehow I find myself sitting in the parking lot for the resort of my date. How did I get here... and who awaits me inside?

Rhodes

Passing the reins of our family's business over to my twin? Check. Building a successful gaming company? Proudly done. My love life? Laughable. I put all my focus in developing my game and company which left little time for dating. When my friend tells me about the auction he'd been working on, I'm curious. What could the auction bring me?

*For my Family and Friends for all your support.
I love you.*

Chapter 1
TREVOR

Will I always be alone? I curse myself as I turn away from yet another guy at the club Eliot's dragged me out to. Sure, the guy's flirting game is on point. Mine? Ha. That's laughable. I have zero game. None. What's a guy to do when you stare at him like he's an alien from outer space?

Ugh. I don't even know why I agreed to Eliot's scheme. We'd be having more fun raiding dungeons with the guild on *King's Ransom* rather than being here. Okay, so sure, I can't get laid and lose my v-card on a game, but a shy, introvert like me won't cut it at the clubs either. That requires a level of trust I just don't have in me.

Rolling my eyes at myself, I glance around the club, looking for Eliot. My eyes trail along the mass of exposed skin and gyrating muscles of sexy men all over the dance floor before they land on my best friend. He's sandwiched between two beef cakes, grinding out the time of his life. Ah, to have it so easy in social situations. I wish I had his charisma sometimes, if only to rid myself of this shyness that's part of my existence.

Eliot finds me looking at him and cocks a brow. I nod my head toward the doors while tugging my phone from my pocket, showing him I'm planning to head out. He frowns, pointing to himself, and I shake my head, letting him know he can stay. No need to invite him to my pity party when he's having a good night. He up-nods to me and puts his hand to his ear, telling me to call him. With a last nod, I break eye contact and turn toward the doors.

I open the ride share app and call for a car, happy to see one is only five minutes away. I slither around a pair of men kissing and groping each other against one of the high-top tables. Skirting the dance floor, I pop out of the club doors into the entry. The guy at the counter gives me a friendly wave as I duck out onto the street to await my ride.

After a cute little blue four-door sedan pulls up, I check the tags and hop into the back with a deep sigh. The driver looks at me in the rearview mirror and I wave him off with a wan smile before glancing out the window. One of these days, I'll figure out how to be social.

Well, it's not like I don't know how, per se. Get me behind my computer screen and I've got no issues talking to people, whether I know them or not. Hiding behind my monitor levels the playing field. Sure, people can judge me across the miles, but I can't see them doing so. Everything just seems easier that way.

I hold back another sigh, not wanting to get the driver's attention like the sad sack I am. No sense in more judgement if I can avoid it. He's got some soft music playing and the ride's a comfy one. As he pulls up to my apartment building, I glance toward him with as much of a smile as I can muster right now. "Thanks for the ride."

He nods as I get out of the car and I up my tip a bit as he drives off. I rub my fob against the plate next to the door to let myself into my building. After entering my small studio apartment, I inhale the scent of an ocean breeze from my wall plugin and feel every muscle in my body relax as the door clicks shut behind me. I flip the locks and kick off my shoes to the rack next to it. Home, sweet freaking home. Honestly, there's no better place for me.

I strip the tight black t-shirt I'd worn to the club over my head as I cross the open plan set up to my gaming rig by the bay windows. I stab the power button with my finger, letting the computer light up and all my gadgets come online. My dual monitors flicker to life. The soft whir of the fans kicking in does even more to soothe my soul as I head toward the bathroom tucked away under my open-air loft.

With a twist of the knob, I get the water to heating. Then I work the skinny jeans clinging to me down my legs before kicking them toward the hamper next to the doorway. My boxer briefs follow the way of the pants before tugging off my socks and tossing them into the basket. I do a little shimmy as both make it into the hamper as if I'm playing a game of basketball. Got to have fun where you can find it sometimes.

As steam rolls over the glass door, I reach in to add some of the cold water till it's just this south of boiling me alive and step into the spray. I turn my back to the water, tilting my head and shutting my eyes. The warmth seeps into my muscles as the water sluices down my skin to the drain below. For the moment, I revel in the familiar that surrounds me and allow my rueful thoughts float into the ether. I can deal with them another night.

I give myself another few moments under the spray before grabbing my shampoo and body wash to cleanse the stink from the club off my skin. No one wants to take that to bed by themselves, or at least, I don't. Feeling I'm as clean as can be, I shut off the knobs. After I grab the towel hanging on the shower door bar, I dry myself off, wrapping the towel around my wet curls like a turban.

I open the closet door connecting to the bathroom and step inside, dragging some clean briefs and a pair of pajama pants from a drawer and slipping them on. I snag a t-shirt from a hanger, letting it dance precariously against the metal rail with a rattle from the momentum before it settles back into place. Time for some actual good fun.

I pad barefoot through my apartment and pull my big rolling chair out from under my desk and sink into it. Tucking my feet underneath me, I wiggle the mouse to wake my sleeping giant from the screensaver and open the chat server for my guild. My heart gives a little zing as my sight narrows in on a name I hoped to find tonight. StarGazer.

I grin to myself as I pop a message into the chat window.

> Hey guys. How's it hanging tonight?
> — Aravar

I double-click the icon to start the game on my other screen, watching as a couple of people answer back. One of them acts the part of a smartass and says, 'to the left'. I shake my head with a laugh, quite entertained by my guildmates' shenanigans. It's a wonderful group of people, all either LGBT+ or an ally.

A lot of times, you hear how toxic the gaming community can be, and that's true. Sometimes, you just have to find your people. I was ecstatic to see a game being touted as LGBT+ friendly and the developers and moderators backing up their statements. Our guild echoes those statements, so I know in this, I'm in a safe space. We're quick to boot people looking to stir up that kind of drama. We deal with it enough IRL. Don't need that shit in-game, too.

As my character finishes loading into his house in the game, a message pops up from StarGazer.

> Much better now. Didn't think I'd see you tonight.
> — StarGazer

A smile crosses my face, and I chuckle at his message. I'd told them this afternoon that I planned to head out with Eliot tonight, who they all know as our illustrious leader, RiverRager. My fingers fly over the keys as I type back.

> Their company just didn't compare with yours.
>
> Aravar

I tag a winky face on to the end and start my character to crafting. See? Game for days when I'm online. Why can't I do this with people face to face? I've got no effing clue, but something within me freezes.

I shove the negative thoughts back from my mind again as I focus on the chat and my game. This is my time to be myself and not wallow in the loneliness that surrounds me.

I set my character to make some new armor sets I'd gotten the recipes for before getting out of my chair. Padding into the kitchen, I nab a coke from the fridge and the bag of white cheddar popcorn from the basket on top. Settling back in my seat with my snack, I pop the tab on the can and guzzle some down before opening the bag with a pop. A new message on my chat greets me.

> Well, I'll count my lucky stars you think that.
>
> StarGazer

Bless all the little baby gay hearts all over the world, this guy is just too sweet. His words make me swoon a bit in my seat as I think of how to reply to him. Our flirting game has always been fun. Can't say I hate it, not one freaking bit.

> You be sure to do that. Count each one carefully.
> — Aravar

StarGazer answers with a wink emoji as one of our guildmates asks for help with a quest line he's on. I stop crafting and we all group up to help him get the difficult quest out of the way. We cut off the flirtatious banter going on between us while we focus in on the mission. As we wrap up the main boss fight and divvy up the loot with random rolls, I yawn and glance over at the clock to see how late it's gotten. Three a.m. Need to grab some shuteye. I teleport back to my home base and hit the button to logout while letting my guildies know I'm heading out for the night. Of course, no night is complete without a last message to StarGazer.

> Until the stars shine again.
> — Aravar

I wait for his answer before I power off my machine and crawl into bed, letting thoughts of an imaginary future with an imaginary man carry me off to sleep.

Chapter 2
RHODES

> And sunlight hides from our gaze.
>
> Person's Name

I don't know what it is about the little spitfire healer from my game that gets me, but he snatches my attention every time he logs on. Tonight was no exception. I'd just been about to log off for the night when his name popped online. Even knowing I've got an early morning, I couldn't help but to stay online longer to talk to him.

I sign off the game when he does and blow out a breath. I've got to get this little crush under control. It's not like I can do anything about it. None of the people in my guild know I run the *King's Ransom* MMORPG we all play, and I'd really like it to stay that way. I enjoy the way they treat me as if I'm just another player. I don't need them kissing up to me, thinking they're going to get some unique shit just from knowing me.

That may be wrong to think of all the guys in the guild, but I've seen it happen in others. Add to the fact I like the people I'm running around with, I want nothing to jeopardize that. So even meeting or doing anything real with my online flirt, Aravar, is not happening. Just got to get over that.

I shove my sweats off and my bare body slides against the cool sheets of my king size bed. I glance over the left side and yet again wish for a body to lie there, for some person to curl around and bury my face in the nape of their neck as I fall asleep. Tonight is not that night. I shut my eyes and force myself to relax and seek the oblivion of darkness.

❤ · ❤ · ❤

I scribble my signature across the line at the bottom of the page, slide the document into the file folder, and set it in the outbox on my desk. It's been a long day of paperwork and getting things ready for the upcoming launch of the game expansion. My teams have put in a lot of work into the first full expansion and I'm hopeful for an explosion of new gamers to flock to the game with the new content. Time will tell, but either way, I want to make sure we well compensate the teams for all their hard work.

I rub my eyes with the heels of my hands for a moment as a soft rapping comes at my office door. Looking up from my work, my assistant pops the door open to step inside. "I'm cutting you off. You're going to be late."

I frown and look at the clock, seeing it's only six in the evening. It's not like I've got anything to run home to. For the past few years, my heart and soul have been building my company and video game from the ground up. A lot of smaller companies get swallowed up by the bigger ones and I've been fighting tooth and nail to compete with more well-known titles in the MMO industry.

With a raised brow, I look back at Regina in confusion. "Late for what?"

My assistant tidies up my desk before grabbing the files in the outbox to take to her desk to deal with. She settles an exasperated look at me with a shake of her head. "Your dinner with Dean at seven? I've only reminded you twice this afternoon."

I groan and drop my head to my desk like a drama queen. I'd totally forgotten I'd set up to catch up with my best friend tonight. We'd both been busy with our own launches, so it'd completely slipped my mind. Again. *Oops*. I lift my head and reach to shut my laptop down to slide it into my bag to take home. "What would I do without you?"

She laughs and shakes her head at me as she backs toward the door. "Lose your mind, more than likely."

I tilt my head to acknowledge she's probably right in that case. She was one of my first hires when I built my team and she's been worth her weight doubled in gold, maybe even triple. Best hire ever. "That's plausible."

I stretch, feeling the muscles tight in my back pull against the movement and groan. Regina stops to look at me with a frown on her face. "After this launch, you need to take a vacation. Or at least some kind of break. You're looking kind of tired there."

I shake my head to her as I sling the strap of my laptop bag over my shoulder and come around my desk to head to the door behind her. "No rest for the wicked. Got to prep for the next content release."

I lock my office door behind us as we enter her area of the office suite. She lays a hand on my arm to stop me from walking away. "No, you're going to take a break. Both you and the teams have earned it. The devs will be busy working through any random bugs which we always know come with releases like this, anyway."

I sigh and shake my head. "Regina…"

The shake of her head cuts me off as she retorts, "Rhodes, it's not up for discussion. You're going to burn yourself out."

I fight the urge to roll my eyes. At least she cares enough about my mental health. I've got to give her that. "I'm not agreeing to anything, but I promise I'll think about it. Will that work?"

Regina rolls her eyes with a put-upon sigh and waves her hand at me as she removes it from my arm. "I guess that'll have to do."

Apparently, I'm the only one fighting such outward shows of emotion this evening. At her agreement, I give her a smile and move toward the office door. "You're the best. See you on Monday."

She nods her head. "Have a good weekend, Rhodes."

I make my way from the building and outside to my waiting car. As I slide into the backseat and greet my driver, I settle into the plush leather seat and turn my gaze out the window, allowing my mind to filter over thoughts of all that could go wrong with the launch to come as the car eases its way through traffic toward my home so I can change to meet Dean.

❦·♥·❦

My car arrives at the restaurant right at seven and I breathe a sigh of relief. I'm on time. I really hate being late to things and having people wait on me. It's my fault for forgetting, so no reason to inconvenience others with my own issues. I stride quickly toward the door and slide inside in time to see Dean stepping up to the hostess stand. The hostess is shaking her head to my friend as I call out to him. "Dean."

His dark blond head swings in my direction, allowing his hazel eyes to settle on mine and crinkle in the corners as he smiles. "Looks like we both made it on time tonight."

I laugh at his words and glance at the hostess as I reach them. "I've got a table for two, Trisha."

The brunette gives me a blinding smile as she recognizes me and grabs two menus from the stacker hooked to the side of the podium. "Of course, Mr. Williamson. If you'll both follow me, your table is ready."

I pat Dean on the back in greeting as we both turn to follow the short woman as she sways her way through the tables to one along the side of the restaurant with the windows facing the park next door. I may come here a bit too much. Trisha not only knows me by name but also my table preference. At least I'm not dining alone tonight. We both thank her as we sit, and she lays down our menus.

Looking across the table at my friend, I ask, "So, how have you been? We've both been a bit too busy to catch up much over the phone."

He laughs and settles into his chair as he flips open the menu. "That might be a bit of an understatement. Prepping for the launch of Carousel's auction made things hectic."

Perking a brow at his words, I'm curious by the mention of the auction he'd not told me about. "I'm assuming Carousel is the dating app you've been working on, but an auction? I must have missed you talking about that."

Dean takes a sip from his water glass before answering me. "Yeah, they've teamed up with the Smooth Getaways travel agency to raise money for charity that helps homeless LGBT+ youth. It's a sweet set up if I say so myself. Some people put themselves up for auction for weekend getaway dates at LGBT+ friendly resorts. Others bid on them. Half of the proceeds will go to the charity and the rest is toward the date, I believe."

I perk a brow, but the server steps up to the table and we both take turns placing our orders and handing our menus over. As the server steps away, I focus my attention back on Dean. "We definitely need more things like that in the world."

He nods with a wry smile on his face. "I can't agree with you more on that. And you? Big launch coming up soon, right?"

I don't want to show it, but the idea of the auction has me intrigued. After all, Regina said I need a vacation, right? Food for thought. I tuck that tidbit into the back of my mind and turn my attention to the question he'd asked.

I nod my head. "Yes, next week, in fact. I'm really excited about the company hitting this milestone and I'm working hard to make sure it's not only a success for me and my teams but also well celebrated by both the staff and the players."

"What sort of celebration are you planning?"

"Well, for starters…"

I delve into my launch plans, telling him all about the update, all while dreams of a potential true love awaiting me at a trip destination dance in my head.

♥ · ♥ · ♥

The car lets me off at the front door of my townhouse and waits while I climb the steps and let myself inside before it drives off. I shut the door and turn to face the living area. A single lamp dimly lights the room, one I'd left on knowing I'd be coming home after dark. Aside from that, nothing but silence and the soft hum of the air conditioning greets me.

It's moments like this that get to me. When I'm busy at work or gaming with my friends, I can ignore the fact no one is around, that I don't have someone to celebrate my wins with. But in silence like this? I sigh at my thoughts and make another wish for a partner to walk this life by my side. Perhaps Regina isn't wrong. Maybe I need more than a vacation.

With the company taking off, do I have the time now? Can I take a step back and work on my personal life? Even Dean pointed out during dinner how we don't meet up like we used to.

I glance into my study where my desktop computer sits. I could shove away the loneliness and lose myself in the game with the others, but right in this moment, that seems more like a band aid rather than a healing salve for my soul.

I walk away from my study, and head upstairs to get ready for bed. Perhaps tomorrow, I'll look at that auction. We've all got to start somewhere, right?

Chapter 3
TREVOR

"Oh, my man, those guys were so fucking hot together. And getting to be a part of that? Mmm... warms my little gay heart to remember it."

I plop down on the couch and switch my phone to the other ear so I can prop my elbow up on the arm to listen to Eliot drone on and on about his recent hookup with the two bears from the nightclub I'd left him dancing at. My best friend is a proud manslut and I might be slightly envious of his ability to be so social and outgoing. Okay, so it's probably more than slightly. Being shy is kind of becoming hazardous to my health, I think.

His words draw a laugh from me as I shake my head at his antics. "Lots of new spank bank material, huh?"

He groans like a porn star, making me roll my eyes. "Soooo much new material. I might be good for a while."

I grin to myself before responding, "So, like a week?"

"You know it, baby cakes. So, what happened to you last night?"

This time, I'm the one groaning and it's most definitely not the porn star type. "Me. I'm what happened. I'm always what happens."

Silence fills the line for a moment, and I pull the phone from my ear to check that the call didn't drop. Still seeing it connected, I put it back to my ear just as Eliot answers. "Maybe we need to try something new, and I've got just the idea."

Eliot's my best friend and I love the guy to the ends of the Earth, but I cringe, wary of what suggestion he's about to make. He knows I'm not a guy for surprises or for new things. I abhor change. Absolutely loathe it. "Do I even want to ask?"

I'm seeing him coming up with something like speed dating—that's a nope from me—or a singles' meet up. Eliot chuckles in my ear. "Oh, it's not that bad. I promise. What about a blind date of sorts? Where it's just you and him, one-on-one, rather than picking from a crowd."

I open my mouth to deny the suggestion, but then close it, stopping to let the idea percolate in my mind. Eliot sits in the quiet with me as I think over it before musing aloud to myself, not even thinking about him hearing my thoughts. "Logically, it's not too bad. It's at least a guaranteed date as long as the other guy shows up. I'm usually pretty good about not spilling food on myself, so I don't have to worry about that."

Eliot jumps in on my thought train. "Yes, exactly. And somewhere with fewer people, though obviously still public for safety reasons. It'll be way less pressure on you."

Perhaps his idea has merit, but then I think about

how I'm kind of an outlier for the people I usually see surrounding my best friend and cringe again. "It'd have to be someone I could gel with. A lot of your friends are…"

I cut myself off, not wanting to offend someone I don't know, especially behind their back. That's just wrong on so many levels. Plus, I have my own issues with peopling, which might skew my sense of others, and his friends are perfectly normal people. Eliot scoffs in my ear. "I'm going to ignore that, but I'm not thinking of the type of blind date where me or someone else sets you up with someone we know. I heard about this auction coming up. The form just launched for sign-ups, and I think it could be good for you."

All I'm able to do is blink. Did he really just suggest I go on a date with some absolute stranger? I mean, yeah, his other friends I consider nuts, but at least he can vouch for them. Apparently, I'm silent too long as Eliot's voice is loud in my ear. "Trevor? You okay there?"

I splutter before squeaking out, "You want me, the ultimate shy introvert, to go out with some totally unknown guy? *Me?*"

Eliot snickers at my dramatics and I'm sure shaking his head at the same time. "Yes, but it's all above board. The site details out all the security checks they'll go through and everything. It's a legit dating app and a legit travel company. Bonus points: half of the proceeds go to a charity to help homeless LGBTQ+ kiddos. So, wins all around for everyone."

I pull my phone from my ear and switch it to speaker before laying down across my couch and staring up at the white popcorn ceiling. "That all sounds well and good, but I don't know. It's just one date, right?"

Eliot hums before slowly answering. "Well… it's more like a weekend thing, as it's a travel getaway."

And there it is, the flaw in his plan. With a roll of my eyes, I turn my head to the side to look at my phone to be sure it picks up the incredulousness in my voice. "A weekend trip away with a stranger and you think that's *my* cup of tea? Geez, Eliot, what the hell have you been smoking tonight? I swear to all that's holy, you're high as a freaking kite!"

My words only make Eliot burst out into laughter. "Nah, and I'm not drunk either, before you go there. But it'll be good for you. It's one way to force you out of your comfort zone without an easy way to run home before the night can even truly get started."

I scoff at his words and don't even deign to respond about how easily I run away. It's not like I can deny his words. I do it all the time. I chew on my bottom lip as he speaks again. "Look. You're doing this, I've decided. So, either you can sign yourself up, or I can. Just know that if I do it, you won't be able to change any of the answers to the questionnaire that I put in."

I close my eyes and take a deep breath, reminding myself over and over that he's my best friend, that I love him, and murder is illegal. After about ten times, I might start to believe the words. "Fine. Send me the link and I'll do it."

"You've got till Monday morning or I'm doing it for you."

Oh yay, a weekend full of anxiety. Just what I need. "Fine. I've got to check on my work schedule for release week. I'll call you later."

"Love you, you know that, right?"

I grab my phone and hold it in front of my face with my finger hovering over the end call button. "Yeah, I know. Love ya too, pain. Talk to you later."

Eliot hangs up, and I let the phone fall to rest upon my chest.

***

I log off the game from my moderator account and stare at the screen, wondering if I should log in to talk to the guild for a while. It's been a long weekend with the auction weighing on my mind. Now, it's Sunday night and if I don't have the application done by morning, Eliot will follow through with his promise of signing me up.

Thinking of my friend StarGazer, my heart flip-flops in my chest. What if the guy I meet is as cool as him? That would be okay.

With a sigh, I pull up the Carousel site and choose the option for being auctioned. As I put in my info, I wonder. What am I getting myself into?

Chapter 4
RHODES

After dinner with Dean learning about the auction, I did what I'd promised Regina I'd do, think about taking a break. It's been a while since I'd gone on a vacation, not since I'd launched my gaming company, so I'm overdue one. The problem is, I don't want to go alone. That's really what's intriguing to me about the auction.

Having come from a very influential family with a well-known name and having built up such a strong gaming company, I know I'm on a lot of families' bachelor lists. That's not vanity, it's truth. It's just how those types of social circles work, as how my mother acts each time I go home can attest to. It's all about settling down and starting a family like I'm a 50s housewife. I can hear her voice now. *'Even gay men can settle down and have kids these days, James Rhodes Williamson.'*

Look, I've got nothing against people who want to have kids, but right now, that's just not my style. That could change later or with the right partner if it was a choice we made together, but right now? No, thank you.

Still, as I sit in the quiet of my home contemplating playing with the guild, I'm wondering how fuller my life could be with someone by my side. Screw it, I'm going for it. It kills two birds with one stone and I can feel them out on how they'd get along with me if they knew who I was. Just got to keep some personal details out of it for a while.

With a plan in mind, I pull up the auction site and tap the button to sign up as a bidder. Let's do this.

❤ · ❤ · ❤

Launch weeks are absolutely insane, and this one is no different. We hit the road running Tuesday morning with the release and it's been non-stop action for the entire company, from me to the developers, to our community moderators.

By the end of the day on Friday, we're all exhausted and I'm thanking them all in a video call for their amazing work. I know it's not done, but we're through the worst of the rush and now it's up to the coders to do what they do best and fix any remaining bugs cropping up. I end the call and settle back in my seat with a heavy sigh. Thank fuck for amazing people, that's all I can truly say at this point.

A tapping sounds at my office door before it cracks open, and Regina pokes her head in. "Good meeting, boss. I think the teams will all love their celebration gifts when they get them next week."

I give a tired smile at her words and hope they're true. A lot of employers these days like to complain about their crew not wanting to work, but I've not found that to be true about my teams. Bonuses go a long way as everyone has bills to pay. Treat people well and they'll do the same for you. Many people in charge of companies have forgotten that fact.

I've had some investors try to strong arm me on my pay policies, but I've told them as professionally and as politely as I could to take a long walk off a short pier. Thankfully, those incidents have been few because I made it known at the onset of investing how I was going to run the company, so they knew all that stuff from the word go.

Regina plops herself down in one of the two blue armchairs in front of my desk and pulls out her tablet. "Ready to wrap up so you can go home and get some well-deserved rest? I'm pretty sure you've not slept well all week, making sure you put all the fires out."

That's putting it mildly. No doubt my blue eyes are bloodshot from just how little sleep I've gotten this week. Tonight calls for a crash-and-burn session with no alarm set. I nod and wave my hand at her. "Yes, please. It's definitely a dinner and bed night for me."

She chuckles before flipping open her notes app and begins giving me the rundown of things I didn't know about for today because it wasn't something I'd had to deal with. I nod periodically as she talks until she's going over the last bit about my personal emails and my attention focuses more on her words. "Last thing on my list is one I'm not sure if it's spam or not. It was a notification about an auction opening for bids?"

I sit up straighter in my chair. With the launch, I'd completely forgotten all about the auction and the future weekend trip. "That's for the trip I told you Monday I'm considering going on. It's a date auction for a weekend getaway that benefits LGBTQ+ homeless youth, so I signed up as a bidder."

Everything in me tells me I'm making the right decision to take part in this auction. Through every step of running my business, my gut instincts haven't led me wrong. Can't see it doing so with this.

Regina hums and ticks it off with her stylus as I continue. "Just in case, can you set up a reminder text for tomorrow afternoon at two p.m. for me to log on and bid?"

She nods and makes a note of my words before closing the case on her tablet. "Will do. Now, go home. We're all done here. I'll order your favorite takeout and have it scheduled for delivery when you're almost home."

This woman, I swear. Life. Saver. I give her a warm smile. "You're my favorite."

She heads for the door with laughter falling from her lips. "As I'll remind you when it's time for a pay raise."

My laughter joins hers as I stand and put my stuff together and head out.

Dinner meets me at home and after stuffing my face with delicious, blackened shrimp Alfredo, I tumble into bed, falling asleep as soon as my head hits the pillow.

♥·♥·♥

Don't forget to place your bid. Good luck, boss!

Regina

The text from my assistant comes right on time as I settle down at my computer, preparing to log onto *King's Ransom* to join my guild for some afternoon raids. I pause and pull up the email instead. Even though I know it sounds like a good idea, I stop with my cursor hovering over the link.

I don't normally deal with nerves, but this is a totally new situation for me. I rarely go in blind without having assessed all the risks, and it's hard to do that when I don't know who I'll be bidding on. Dean said it's hit or miss with pictures as they were encouraging blind listings, but there would be questions and answers for the bidders to look at to get a sense of the date they're bidding on.

Thinking about the homeless kids my bid could help, I click on the button. If nothing else, it's a trip and hopefully a good one. I filter the results to show ones that are near me, since I don't want to travel too far and start perusing the listings.

My scrolling finger gets a workout as I look at several profiles and save the ones I'm contemplating. Then I get to another listing, and I have to stop. The profile states that it's a gay male, but that's not what stops me. It's the question about qualities in a partner which grabs my attention, or rather, the guy's answer to it. *Must love video games.* Well, if that one isn't up my alley.

I don't even stop to think about it. I push the button to submit a bid and put in several thousand dollars. It's for a good cause, after all. The little cursor icon turns into a spinning wheel and hovers over my screen as the site processes my submission.

I wiggle in my seat, as if anxious that it's taking so

long when it's only been a few seconds. The screen ticks over to a new page, thanking me for my bid and telling me they will alert winners via email next week.

Maybe it's childish, but I cross my fingers on both hands and say a tiny prayer to any deity listening. *Please let this be my turn.*

❤・❤・❤

To say the past few days since I'd placed my bid had been easy? Understatement. Trying to focus on my work would be a bald-faced lie. While I normally let my assistant handle all my emails, I had turned the notifications on my phone to show them for now.

I open my business email to compose a new one to the head of the development team when my phone dings from the side of my desk. Snatching up the device, I see the notification I'd been waiting for, the email from Carousel. I open it nervously to see what's inside.

> Congratulations! You're the winning bidder of a blind date trip to the Pinnacle Resort in the Blue Ridge Mountains of Virginia. Darcy and the team from Smooth Getaways will be in contact with you and your date to help plan your trip. Enjoy and have a great week!

I almost fist pump the air but catch myself. I can't stop the wide grin that crosses my face, though. Here's to hoping for a great first 'date'.

Chapter 5
TREVOR

The auction had alerted me about the winning bidder, and I had a choice to contact them before our date, but any time I tried, I chickened out. It's easy to do that over a text message rather than in person, so here's to hoping the trip goes well.

Eliot put me on the plane himself. He said he wasn't taking any chances of me running back home and claiming I'd missed my flight. He knows me all too well, I'm afraid. Maybe it's time to get a new best friend, one who doesn't quite see me so much. I kid. I wouldn't trade him in for the life of me.

So that's why I'm standing here on the front steps of a large mountain lodge, just staring at the doors as if they'll reach out and grab me. I'm a bit frozen to go inside. I've made it this far. The universe can shove me the rest of the way.

As I'm building up the nerve to take the next steps, a deep, masculine voice sounds behind me moments before a body collides into my back. "Yes, I know. *I know*, Regina. I'm on vacation. I just got to the resort and the phone's going... oof."

Arms wrap around me from behind as I pitch forward, almost falling from the impact. A phone clatters to the porch and a tinny voice calls out something inaudible. As I steady my breathing from almost smacking my face on the weathered wood flooring, that same voice speaks again. "I'm so sorry. I wasn't paying attention to where I was going."

Being hauled back against the hard lines of a male body is what I'd like to consider a good time, and the sensation of it hits me full force. I like it as much as I imagined I would. As my feet steady beneath me, the arms fall away and I step forward and turn around to look up, *way up*, at the tall man who'd saved me from a scraped face.

The man is absolutely gorgeous. He's a head taller than me—consummate twink standing at only 5'8"—with deep blue eyes like the depths of the deep ocean and close-cropped blond hair. A gentle smile curves his lips on a tanned face as our eyes meet. A shiver races down my spine, but the rest of me freezes. I'm supposed to say something back, but my brain doesn't want me to make words work. My mouth opens and closes as I try to say something, *anything*, to this man.

The smile on his face turns upside down as he takes a step away from me. I want to reach out and grab him, tug him back into my body as if he belongs there, but that's stupid, right? I've never been so drawn to a stranger before, but something about this man just calls to me. The fact I'm here to meet a blind date for a weekend isn't even a blip on my radar right now. He looks away toward the door. "Again, I apologize. Hope I didn't hurt you."

He makes for the door, striding inside before my words squeak out my throat seconds too late as the door closes between us. "It's okay..."

My head flops back on my neck as I look up at the porch ceiling overhead, staring at the white boards that match the floor. Can I be any weirder to people? What is my date going to think of me? Oh crap, my date. I shake my head at myself and contemplate pulling my phone out of my pocket and heading home, or to another hotel, or hell, to another planet. Ghosting my date would be significantly better than forcing him to deal with my awkwardness.

Screw this. Tugging my phone out of my pocket to call up a ride-share, I find a text notification waiting for me.

Eliot: You're not allowed to bail on your date. Go meet this guy. Think of the homeless kids, my man. You can do this. Love you.

I laugh under my breath at my best friend's antics. The man sure knows me well. Pushing the power button to darken the screen, I shove it back into my pocket. I take a deep breath and hold it for a few moments before letting it out with an audible whoosh. "I can do this."

With a firm mental shake at myself, I take a step toward the doors and out of my comfort zone. Here goes nothing.

I pull open the doors and step off the hardwood porch onto the plush carpet, feeling the soles of my tennis shoes sink into the pile beneath my feet. The lushness doesn't stop there as I'm surrounded by several sitting areas with armchairs and couches designed to make a body just drown in the comfort waiting on them. The muted shades of tan, blue, and green spread throughout the room, giving me a sense of comfort as I take it all in, all the way to the check-in counter where the man from outside stands talking with the attendant waiting on him.

I shift my weight from foot to foot and step to the side of the doors so I'm not blocking the way in. I could be a normal person and wait in line behind him, but then he might see me again and I might make him even more uncomfortable. From the maps they sent me of the resort, I know the place is rather large, so the likelihood of running into him again after this is slim. Best not to make things even more awkward. I sidle to the side, hiding behind one of the potted trees spaced out over the room and wait for him to be shown to wherever he's staying.

As I wait, the door opens and another single man steps through. This one isn't nearly as attractive as the man at the desk. I study him from my hiding place as he approaches the front desk and gets in line before my gaze starts ping-ponging between the two of them. Could either of them be my date?

Before I can answer myself, a waiting porter leads away the guy who ran into me and they disappear out the rear French doors at the back of the lodge. I turn my gaze back to the other guy as he steps up to the desk and I make my way from behind the plant and go to stand behind him. Nothing about this guy makes me as nervous as the other guy did just by being so dang gorgeous.

As another waiting porter leads the second guy from the lodge, I take a step forward as a woman with the name tag, Laura, smiles at me. "Well, hey there. Welcome to Pinnacle Resort. How can I help you today?"

I give a bit of a smile in return to her greeting. "Um, hi. My name's Trevor Maines. I'm here for the Sweetheart Escapes getaway?"

I'm hoping I got that part right. The agent had told me what to say when I checked in, but my nerves about going on this trip totally blanked out my memory and I, idiot that I am, didn't write it down. She beams at me as she types on her computer with a nod. "Of course, Mr. Maines. I have you right here. You just missed the other half of your party, so you'll meet them at the treehouse."

I glance toward the double doors they had led the man out of mere moments ago. So that *was* him. Well, at least I'll make it through the weekend unscathed. Had it been that first guy, bailing out was still an option. No sense in torturing either of us with my awkwardness, or worse. I let my gaze travel back to the hostess and attempt a decent smile, as if I'm really looking forward to this weekend. "Sure, um, that's fine."

I've never been a big fan of peopling, much less done a lot of traveling, so I'm not sure what to say in this scenario. I swallow and tap my toes, glad the carpet doesn't make any sound to give my fidgeting away to the woman. She looks away from the computer as she slides a slim folder about the size of a trifold brochure across the glossy desk surface to me. "There's already a card on file for the room, so I won't need one from you. Inside is your keycard that works for access to the treehouse and for any amenities and for the main lodge areas after hours."

She waves to another one of those porters as he steps

up to the counter. "Carlos here will take you to the treehouse and handle your bags. Is there anything else I can help you with?"

I suppose asking her for help with an escape plan if this whole weekend backfires on me is out of the scope of her job description, so I shake my head as I reach up and nab the folder from the desk. "Um, nope. That all sounds good. Thanks."

She gives me another cordial smile. "We're glad to have you with us, Mr. Maines. Enjoy your weekend and let us know if you need anything."

Her gaze darts from me to Carlos before she addresses him. "He's booked into the Summit, please."

As her gaze trails back to me, I nod to her as I step away, turning to face a smiling Carlos. He steps forward to grab the small suitcase I'd set at my feet. "Hi, Mr. Maines, was it?"

I dip my head in acknowledgement of his words. "Um, yeah. Nice to meet you, Carlos."

"Nice to meet you too, sir. Want me to grab that bag as well?"

He motions to the messenger bag strapped across my body and I shake my head. "Nah, I've got this one."

He grins, and motions toward the doors all the other men had gone through. "Then follow me and I'll take you to the Summit."

He leads me outside to a golf cart parked off to the side, and I climb onto the passenger side. He stows my suitcase in a cage on the back and hops into the driver's seat. As he drives, he talks about the resort, but all I can think about is one thing. Who awaits me at the end of this journey?

Chapter 6
RHODES

The lead up to the treehouse was amazing. It's set next to a drop-off in a large tree. A bridge from the cliff's edge leads out to the treehouse's private deck, which has holes cut out for the tree branches to grow through. I can't see anyone else for miles, giving me a sense of being alone on this mountain.

The entire cabin has a rustic-meets-homey vibe. The wooden walls give the visitor the feel of a cabin in the woods, but the furnishings make it feel like home, from the luxurious looking sectional couch to the plush bedding on each of the beds.

I'd tipped the porter before he left me alone. Apparently, I'm the first to arrive, but that's okay. I look around the treehouse they'd assigned us to, noting the two separate bedrooms. If we're not attracted to each other, at least we don't have to sleep in the same bed or one of us have to bunk on the couch.

With my small tour done, I sink onto the plush tan

leather couch and stare out the window at the gorgeous view. Miles of mountain range and treetops are visible from our high perch—which, according to the porter, the cabin is at the apex of the resort's land and that's why they call it the Summit. Works for me. It's beyond beautiful and if this whole thing goes sideways, I'll at least have one hell of a relaxing view.

My thoughts veer to the man I'd almost bowled over. I'm not sure if I'm hoping the guy is or isn't my date for the weekend. He was adorable as hell and just my type, but he seemed really unnerved by me. I don't want to spend all weekend with a guy who's afraid of me. That doesn't spell good times.

Before I can travel too far down the 'who will he be' path my brain tries to take me on, there's a knock upon the door before it clicks open just enough to allow a voice to ring through the space. "Resort staff and your fellow guest. Are we clear to come in?"

I suppose if they'd just come on in, it could've been awkward if I'd had my birthday suit on. I appreciate the cordiality of the resort and call back. "Come on in."

I sit on the edge of the couch, waiting for my first sight of my date, hoping like hell I'm not about to be disappointed. A man dressed in the resort's uniform steps through first and sets a suitcase next to mine in the entryway. As he steps aside, I hold my breath.

The fates don't disappoint as the small guy from the lodge steps through the door. His brown hair is wind blown, and it flops into his downcast face, hiding the color of his eyes behind not only the unruly bangs, but his eyelids as well. I almost want to order him to look at me, but before the words can cross my lips, he raises his head, pushing his glasses up his nose to stare at me. His jaw drops a bit as recognition flits across his face and flares to life within the deep chocolate brown of his eyes. "It's you."

Damn it all to hell in a handbasket. I really wish the incident on the porch hadn't happened, but not much I can do about that now. I push the thought away as I stand and give him as warm a smile as I can. Hopefully, we can salvage the rest of the weekend. If not? Well, I'll figure something out. I always do. "Hi again. Hope I didn't hurt you when I ran into you."

Yet again, the man just stares at me as if he's seen a fucking ghost and, to be honest, it's getting a little annoying. As my gaze goes to the resort employee where he hovers in the open door, my date finally speaks, or rather squeaks. "No, no. I'm fine. It's okay."

Well, that's progress at least. I nod in acknowledgment of his words before approaching the employee as I slip a folded twenty-dollar bill from my pocket and hold it out to him. "Thanks. Think we have it from here."

The employee thanks me and shuts the door behind him, leaving me alone with the adorable man blinking up at me. He's almost a head shorter than me, making all the protective instincts within me rise, wanting to keep him tucked into my side and safe. Yeah, not doing that right now, so I shove those thoughts to the wayside with all the others and hold my hand out to him. "How about we start over? I'm Rhodes."

He glances down at my hand before a warm, trembling palm slides against my own. He peers up at me through his lashes like a shy deer as he speaks, his voice soft and uneven. "Um, nice to meet you. I'm Trevor."

I'm not sure why he seems so scared of me. I know I'm a big guy, topping out at 6'3" with a modest build, but is that all it is? Shit, I need a game plan here. I give him another smile as I release his hand and head back into the living area to sink onto the couch. I turn my head his direction, but do my level best not to stare at him or even seem like I am. "It's nice to meet you, too. Want to sit down with me for a bit before we settle in for the weekend? I was thinking about maybe us setting some ground rules for how we want the weekend to go will help ease us into things."

A dark brow the same color as his mop of hair rises over the rim of his glasses before he moves further into the cabin and sinks down onto one of the nearby armchairs. A curious look crosses his face. "Ground rules for what?"

I cross one of my legs over my knee and get comfortable before I wave a hand between us. "I know it's difficult for some to share a space with a stranger. You never truly know the person they are at first. Might make sharing some personal details about yourself hard. So, ground rules on how we make the weekend more comfortable for everyone. Like…"

I trail off and think for a moment. I snap my fingers cause I kind of already started with one we could use. "Like no sharing in-depth personal details. For example, we can say what our jobs are about, but leave out titles or even the places we work at."

His head tilts as he studies me before his quiet voice

crosses the space between us. "Like I can say I work remotely because I don't like dealing with people on a good day?"

A bark of laughter spills from me, and I grin at him with a nod. "Yes, things like that. It'll allow us get to know each other a little better and who knows, maybe by the end of the weekend, we might find we're comfortable enough to share more going forward. Or you could decide to tell me to go to hell. Both are viable options."

A hint of a smile curves at the edges of his pale pink lips as he nods his head. "Okay. I like that rule. Um…"

He looks around the space and at the open doorways leading into the bedrooms and the shared bathroom. How a place like this handles plumbing, I've got no idea, but the guy who showed me to the treehouse said it had working plumbing.

I wait for him to look back at me as he continues speaking. "Maybe not sleeping together right off the bat? The thought of it makes me nervous."

I'm glad I had the time to tour the place, so at least I could lay his worries to rest easily enough. I point to the doors on the east side of the room. "Easy enough. The cabin has two bedrooms with queen-size beds. Also, since you mentioned not liking to deal with people, if at any point you need a break to yourself, you've got a space just for you. I promise I won't barge into your bedroom without knocking first."

His shoulders appear to sink a bit as he relaxes at my words. Seeing whatever fear or tension tightening his features since I collided with him ease away makes me feel better, too. Seems my attention to detail gives us more progress. His smile appears as more than a hint this time. "I'd appreciate that."

Hopefully, the last rule in my head doesn't hinder the progress I've made so far. I glance at my watch before dipping my head to him and raising my index finger. "Just one more rule I think we should put into place. No sex for the next twenty-four hours."

Chapter 7
TREVOR

Wait. Did he just say what I think he said? I stare at him as I try to process the words. He's really okay with no sex from the get-go? Most guys, in my experience, as little as it is, want to get straight into it. Granted, those have all been nightclub hook-ups, but even listening to Eliot's stories makes it seem like that's often the case.

I flop against the back of the chair and swallow. "Not that this is an offer, cause I'm just kind of wanting clarification on this. Say we both wanted it, still no sex?"

Rhodes nods his head to me and clasps his hands together on his lap. "Yeah. I think it'll give us both some time to really get to know the type of person the other is without lust making things hazy. It's probably also a good thing to note here that I won't push you for sex over our weekend together. At all. That's not my style. You say no, it's not happening. *Period*."

Holy cripes, I'd already thought the guy extremely attractive, but can he be any more freaking perfect? Being a virgin and facing first times isn't easy for me. And he won't push me on it? Yes, please. I'm all for that. For the first time since we met, I feel a genuine smile come to my face. "Thanks for that. It eases my mind a lot about the weekend."

He grins and a dimple forms on the right side of his mouth. "Great. Glad we've got that sorted. I'll let you pick the first room. I say we both get settled in and then we can meet back here for dinner?"

With a nod, I stand and look at the rooms. "Sounds like a plan. See you soon."

Crossing the room, I grab the handle of my suitcase and wheel it to the nearest bedroom. I'm honestly not picky on what the inside looks like, so random choice it is. As I shut the door behind me, I give a glance into the living area to find a pair of sultry, cerulean blue eyes watching me before the scene disappears behind the closed door.

♠·♥·♠

It didn't take me long to get my things put away in my room. I'd taken out the clothes which needed hanging out of my bag and put them on hangers in the closet, but I left the rest in my bag. We're only here for two nights. There's no need to put my things in the dresser. I'd set my bathroom bag on the dresser top to take with me when I leave my room to drop it off in there, but that's it.

Not wanting to seem like I was in a rush to beat him back out to the shared space, I'd taken the time to appreciate the view from the bay windows in my room. When the travel agent had told me it was a treehouse, I'd not expected to be so high up. Good thing I'm not afraid of heights.

My window showed an expansive view of the tree-covered mountains, and I even spied the glint of water from the lake I knew was part of the resort. I'd pulled my phone out of my pocket and snapped a selfie in front of the window and had sent it to Eliot as proof I hadn't ghosted on my date.

> Why are you texting me instead of sexing up your date?
> Eliot

I chuckle before typing back.

> Oh hush. We're getting settled into our rooms.
> Trevor

I walk away from the window and flop over the bed onto my stomach, propping myself up with my elbows as I watch the dots bounce up and down.

> Rooms? As in 2? Ugh. I was totally hoping for a just-one-bed romance for you.
> Eliot

> OMG, I'm not a RomCom superstar here. No one would watch me if I was.
>
> Trevor

> Like hell they wouldn't. Adorkable little twink like you? Men all over the world would jizz their pants at it.
>
> Eliot

My best friend, people, the moron. I roll my eyes at his antics before checking the clock on the bedside table. Suppose I've been in here long enough. I type a quick last text to Eliot before scrambling off the bed.

> Yeah, sure. If you say so. I'm gonna go see if he's back in the main room. And before you tell me to go sex him up, we're not sexing anything up for the next 24 hours. Byyeee!
>
> Trevor

I put my phone on the charger cord and leave it behind in the room, so I'm not tempted to see what Eliot says to the bomb I dropped on him. The shock no doubt on his face is likely to come through the text message. While his reply is sure to be hilarious, I'm not here to text my best friend all weekend. I'm here to get to know Rhodes.

Before I leave the room, the phone rings. I grab it and take in the name on the screen, Smooth Getaways. It hits me a few seconds later that it's the travel agency. I'd forgotten they were supposed to call after our scheduled arrival. I swipe to accept the call. "Hello?"

A woman's voice sounds over the line. "Good afternoon, Mr. Allen. My name's Darcy and I wanted to check in with you. Make sure everything is going okay so far?"

I sink onto the edge of the bed. "Oh, um, yes, ma'am. It's all good so far. He seems nice."

She chuckles and I hear the customer service smile in her voice as she continues. "Very good, sir. I don't want to keep you long, so if you don't have any issues to report, I'll leave you to your date. Keep in mind, if you feel you need to leave, do so. Just call us, if you could, so we can have it for our records and ensure your continued safety."

I almost want to ask her what they'd do about my safety if they're not on site, but I don't let my pessimistic nature loose on her. She's just doing her job, after all. "I'll do that. Thanks."

She hangs up and I nab my Dopp kit off the dresser before opening the door to escape the room. I drop it off on the bathroom counter before peering around the main living space for my date. I figured he'd be relaxing on the couch again, but he's not there.

I hear a deep humming sound coming from around the corner and I follow it into the kitchen where Rhodes sits on a stool at the island with a piece of white card stock with the Carousel and Smooth Getaways logos up at the top. I clear my throat to let him know I'm there before speaking. "What's that?"

Rhodes spins around on the barstool, holding up the paper. "This? It's the itinerary the travel agency set up for our weekend. A copy of it was in our welcome folder from the resort."

I approach the island and climb up on the stool near him, my gaze falling to the itinerary. "I know they emailed us a copy, but I don't remember a lot."

I bite down on my lower lip, wondering if I should even mention why, as I cast my gaze to the countertop. The deep rumbling of his voice I'm coming to know as comforting is soft upon my ears as he speaks. "What is it?"

I force myself to lift my head to meet his eyes. "To be honest, this whole thing is so far out of my comfort zone, I don't even know where the zone is anymore."

He frowns as his hand falls to rest upon the countertop near mine, yet not touching, almost as if he wanted to reach out and place his hand upon mine, but stopped himself. "If I can ask, why push yourself so far?"

I scratch the back of my neck at his question. It's not like it's one I've not asked myself a billion and one times since I pushed the submit button on the stupid application, but it's not one so easily answered, at least not to a stranger.

As I stare into blue eyes filled with caring, something within me unravels a bit, like maybe I could trust him, just a little. It's almost like I know who he is, but that's silly. Him, I'd definitely remember meeting. I answer with a sigh upon my lips. "Because if I don't, I'll keep letting my fears build up and up, until they become unsurmountable. It already seems as if they are, so I'm trying to push past them. How much of my life will I miss if I don't?"

He stretches out his index finger to run it alongside mine in the barest of touches before he moves his hand away. "Fear can hold us back from so much. I'm glad you didn't let it hold you back from meeting me here."

I give him a small smile. "Yeah, I think I am too."

He chuckles and waves the itinerary. "This says we've got dinner tonight in the main lodge. How about we go down there and get this date started, hmm?"

I hop off the stool and nod. "Yeah, let's do that."

We both head for the door, and hopefully, head for so much more.

Chapter 8
RHODES

As we walked along the gravel path to the main lodge, we talked about the scenery and pointed out things along the way we might want to do the next day. The entire time, though, my heart was breaking for this man. His words about his fears keeping him from living, I hated that for him. While I can't understand it from a fear aspect, being a workaholic as I've been, I understand that fear of missing out.

I can't say I haven't wondered what I've missed over the years that I've dedicated my life to my business. As far as my career is concerned, it's been worth it. Personally? Oh yeah, that's suffered, but just like he's facing his fears and meeting me, I'm facing that deficit in my life and I'm making the changes. It might be a bit too early to wonder if we'll face those together, but I can admit it would be nice to experience it with him. This is a good first step.

I pull open the door and hold it for him, causing a pink flush to seep into his cheeks as he thanks me and slips inside. Gah, the man is just adorable as hell. I might form a bit of a crush on him, but hell, who can blame me?

I follow him inside, allowing the door to shut quietly behind us as I glance around the lodge for where we need to go. The hostess is still at the front desk, and she looks up at our entrance. "Good evening, gentlemen. Anything I can help you with?"

"Yes, we're looking for the restaurant."

She gives us a smile and points toward a set of oaken doors to the right. "Straight through there."

We thank her and move toward the doors. Trevor reaches them first and this time, he holds the door for me. I give him a saucy wink as I step past him. "Why, thank you, cutie."

He stumbles over his own two feet as another blush heats his cheeks. That was on purpose cause he's just so pretty with pink in his cheeks, though this one seems redder than the last, tinting the tips of his ears.

I tear my gaze away from him as the situation in my pants makes them snugger than they already were. I promised the guy no sexy times for twenty-four hours and I need to stick to that. Some light flirting, though? That doesn't count against the rules, so it's still a fair game. Hopefully, it'll be the one he jumps in on at some point. Then I'll know I'm doing the right things here.

That he's been able to talk to me after our initial disastrous run-in speaks volumes about how far he's come. At least, that's my hope. Hard to tell what another person is thinking or feeling sometimes. Wouldn't want to be a mind reader just to figure that out though.

We step up to the host stand and a young man about

twenty gives us one of those cordial, customer service smiles. "Good evening. Hope it's been a good day. Do you have a reservation or are you a walk-in?"

Trevor blinks at him and I recall him saying he doesn't remember much of the plans the agency had made for us, so I answer the host myself. "We should have a reservation. Under either Williamson or…"

I trail off as I glance over at Trevor. "We didn't share last names."

He meets my gaze. "It's Maines. My last name is Maines."

He's got a weird look on his face for just a moment, but he seems to shake it off as he turns back to the host. "Ah yes, a table for two."

The man turns to grab two menus before waving us to follow him. "This way."

I motion for Trevor to lead the way, and we both follow the host as he leads us to a secluded table before a window overlooking the lake in the distance. "Is this one alright?"

I glance over at Trevor, and he nods. I give the host a smile as we both move to take seats at the table across from each other. "This is perfect. Thank you."

The young man sets a menu before each of us. "Your server will be Maisey. Thanks for dining with us this evening."

With a dip of his head, the host leaves us to the seclusion of our little table. Small dividers interspersed with plants and a few feet of space keep the tables distanced enough to give people a sense of privacy. The space was complete with low lighting, set just so to give whoever was sitting at the table a soft glow about their skin, or at least it seems to as I glance over the center of the table at my date.

He's flipped the leather-bound holder open and is looking over the items with a furrowed brow before glancing up at me. "I've never eaten at a place where the menu didn't have prices before. You?"

I open my menu but keep hold of his dark brown gaze as I answer. "A few times, yes."

I let my gaze drop to the words upon the thick, cream paper set into the leather sleeve, hoping he doesn't see I'm not quite being so honest about the number of times. Blame my parents and the circles they keep. The gaming world rarely requires such fancy dining, but being a son of the Williamson family of Williamson Holdings and Investments did.

My family came from old money my grandfather made in investing and I'd originally been the heir to the company. While I had a decent head for business, working for the family firm wasn't where my interest had lain. My twin brother, however, had been all stoked about it. He'd taken over when my dad retired, allowing me the freedom to set up my gaming company.

My elitist parents had, of course, gawped at me wanting to start such a company, but the years of steady growth I'd shown helped them to see it was a brilliant investment.

But those are all details I'm not ready to let Trevor know. So many see the Williamson name or that I'm a CEO and get dollar signs in their eyes. I really don't want the same to happen with Trevor. Is it too much to ask for someone to like me for who I am, not what I'm worth? I hope I'm right, as I've no desire for a loveless marriage to someone just for the name, money, or prestige.

Trevor makes a soft humming sound before settling back in his seat as a young lady with blonde hair tied up in a French knot behind her head and a pair of cat-eye glasses perched on her nose steps up to the table in an all-black uniform. "Good evening, gentlemen. I'm Maisey and I'll be your server for the evening. Is there anything I can start you with?"

I look up at the woman with a smile before glancing over at Trevor with a raised brow. "You see any appetizer you'd like? Glass of wine?"

As I stare at the beautiful man across from me while waiting for his answer, I'm hit with the fervent hope yet again that this weekend goes well. I think I might like to keep seeing him.

Chapter 9
TREVOR

Awkward dinner conversation is, well, awkward. It's why I've always hated the idea of first dates. Still, I can't believe I'm finally on my first real one. Sure, it took an auction and a trip to another state to happen, but it's happening. I sure as hell hope I'm not dreaming, though I'm not sure even my imagination is good enough to conjure up a man who looks as good as Rhodes.

Every time our eyes meet, when I've let them, I get this weird little flutter in the pit my stomach. So far, I'd been attributing it to nerves, but what if all that mess about butterflies in your stomach and zinging touches is real? It's not like Eliot can tell me, as he's all about the hook-up scene. So... what if?

I'm drawn from my thoughts as Rhodes reaches across to touch my fingers resting on the table while calling my name. I tear my gaze away from his blue one to keep from getting lost in those depths again as I peek at the menu once more. "Oh, um. No, I think I'm good with just an entrée and a dessert."

I risk a peek through my lashes at him as he studies me a moment longer before drawing his hand away and turning those ocean blue eyes back upon our server. "Just two waters for now. Then we should be ready to order?"

The question in his tone had him glancing back in my direction, so I nod my head in a simple enough answer. The server addresses us both. "Two waters. I'll get those. Give you guys a few more minutes to look over the menus."

She departs the table, leaving me still shyly glancing through my lashes and Rhodes looking down at his menu. "So, this doesn't seem much like your scene."

Talk about an understatement. A small huff of laughter leaves me and a grin tugs at the edges of my lips before I answer. "Not at all. I'm what you'd call a homebody."

Rhodes taps his finger at an item on the menu before he flips it closed to look back up at me with a smile upon his lips. "Well, not much I can do about the scenery, but perhaps I can make it a bit of an easier night for you."

Color me intrigued. The man is always coming up with some kind of plan in that brain of his, as if all his attention is set on making me feel at ease in his company. I've got to admit, it makes me feel better about this weekend. I don't want to bolt as much right now, but this is me we're talking about. That could crop up at any moment.

I wave a hand his direction. "What's the plan this time?"

He chuckles and a slight tinge of pink highlights the apples of his cheeks as I make him blush for the first time since our meeting. "Figured out I like my plans already, hmm?"

I nod my head. "That's the way it seems to me."

"You wouldn't be wrong with that assumption. I do like laying things out and coming up with workable solutions. So, here's what I propose. First dates are always awkward from what to talk about to how to act. It's all quite tedious, yes?"

I don't really know, but I nod anyway. He can't be too far off the mark, and he's probably had way more first dates than me with the zero on my scorecard. Or my one, I suppose, since I can probably count tonight now.

He gives me a smile before continuing, "How about we play a game of questions? We can ask basic questions about each other, our parts of the world, et cetera. The skies is the limit. If it comes to mind, ask it. We can choose to pass if we want, and we can take turns."

That's not too bad of an idea either. The man is apparently full of ideas. "Sounds good to me. Who goes first?"

"Flip for it? Seems like the only fair solution."

I laugh softly at his words cause I'm pretty sure neither of us was doing much jingling in our pockets as we'd walked here. "Well, I know I'm not carrying any change, so what do we flip?"

Rhodes leans to one side and shoves a hand into his pocket and draws out a single coin. "My lucky quarter. I carry it around in case I ever need some random luck."

I lean against the edge of the table and motion to the quarter in his hand. "I call heads."

He tilts his head to the side before he nods. "Here goes."

He balances the quarter on his thumb and index finger before flipping it up into the air and catching it and enclosing it on the back of his other hand. "Ready?"

With a single nod, my gaze falls to his hand, waiting for him to expose the coin. As he lifts his hand, I see the eagle on the backside of the coin. He chuckles before grabbing the quarter and tucking it back into his pocket. "Looks like I'm going first."

He stops as the waitress steps back to the table. We give her our orders and she leaves us in our peaceful little corner. His eyes return to mine as he taps his chin in thought. "We'll start off easy. What's your favorite color?"

I give a soft laugh of my own. "That's what I was going to ask. Simple enough. Deep green, like an emerald. You?"

We both relax in our seats again before he answers. "No judgement, but purple, like the color of the night sky at twilight where the blue is turning black."

"Hmm, now what to ask for my turn? Since we're here to eat, favorite food?"

He sips his water before answering me. "Tacos. I love a good taco. Might make me a cheap date, but sometimes, simple is just amazing."

I nod my head, cause yeah, that I know. I'm a simple guy with simple likes. "Totally get that. Probably why mine's simple as well. I love a good baked potato, the kind all crusted up with salt on the outside. Toss in some butter, bacon, and cheesy goodness and I've got me a meal right there."

The little spiel on how I take my potato makes me blush and avert my gaze out the window as the sky turns the deep blue of twilight almost to the shade he loves best.

"So, tacos and baked potatoes and we've got the perfect meal for the two of us, huh? I'd say it sounds like a match made in heaven."

I can't help but grin at his words, and inside my head, I kind of hope he's right.

Chapter 10
RHODES

We continued with the silly questions long after the server had brought our dinner and we'd eaten. More were asked, all the way they delivered the cheesecake we'd both admitted was our favorite dessert. Since making my suggestion of the questions, conversation flowed between the two of us. I could keep it going that way, but I've got an urge to see that blush once more. So, I toss out my next question.

"Favorite sex position?"

His fork clatters loudly against the plate as he drops it and stares at me, his cheeks, ears, and even most of his neck flushing a very hot-looking red as he stares at me wide-eyed through the lenses of his glasses. "Wha... Did you just ask that?"

He shoots a quick look around us, even though no one was near enough to overhear our conversation. I give him a mischievous grin. "Just wanted to make sure you were still paying attention and not lost in a lustful haze over this delicious dessert."

He rolls his eyes and shoves a large forkful of the fluffy dessert into his mouth. Can't blame him, really. It's great cheesecake. I follow his motions and take my own, not so large of a bite.

I give the moment time to settle before speaking again. "But for real. This next question is the most crucial for anyone to ask."

He gives me a wary look and carefully sets his fork on the plate, apparently not wanting to drop it a second time if I shock him again. I must admit, his reaction shocks even me, but it could be because of so many things. So, I didn't raise questions about it to make him self-conscious of anything. "Crucial? Really?"

I nod most solemnly to him and lean forward over my plate as I look him in the eyes. "Over or under?"

His brow wrinkles in the center as confusion crosses his pretty face. "Over or under what?"

"The toilet paper roll and how you place it on the holder."

He places his forehead against one hand and shakes his head with a laugh. "Seriously? That's crucial to you?"

"Well, of course it is. There's a right way and a wrong way. I want to make sure we both understand that from the get-go."

More shaking of his head commences, but his eyes glance up to the right before coming back to mine. "I'm an over guy. So, is that the right or the wrong answer?"

"Totally the right answer. Phew. At least that's one fight we don't have to worry about."

He laughs at that. "So, we're on to topics which start

fights, are we?"

I nod as we both finish our dessert and drape our napkins on the table. "Sure. Best to get those out of the way now and save some trouble later. Things like that get a guy into trouble."

He shrugs his shoulders. "That's true. Ready to head back?"

I give an affirmative nod and we both stand, tossing down some bills for tips and chuckling. Even though the resort and trip are all expenses paid, apparently, we both agree on tipping well for services rendered. So many good signs. "So, what's a pet peeve topic of yours?"

We make our way from the restaurant to the back of the lodge, and he seems to think about it. "Hmm. It's not really a pet peeve, but schedules are important. So, morning person or night owl?"

As we step out into the cooling night air with a myriad of stars shimmering overhead, I glance over at him as we walk back to the treehouse. "Well, work means early mornings, but I'm not a fan. I'm a night owl when I can get away with it."

"Good, me too. At least that means you won't throw a pillow at my head for keeping you up."

I place a hand on his arm and draw us to a stop. As his eyes raise to meet mine, I frown. "Someone's done that to you?"

I don't like that at fucking all. No one should assault him just for choosing to stay up late. If they didn't like it, Bluetooth sleep masks are a thing.

He chuckles and pats my hand, still resting on his arm. "It's okay. My very brief first roommate in college had issues. Turned out he was autistic, but his parents had never gotten him diagnosed. We were only together a week before he got a single and I met my best friend Eliot who moved into the room with me."

Well, that takes the wind out of my sails. Can't really get mad at someone with disabilities like that. I shake it off and we walk again. "Okay, that makes a bit more sense. Hopefully, the school got the guy the help he obviously needed."

Trevor shrugs. "Not sure, really. We didn't click as roommates, so I didn't really keep in touch with him. He just emailed me an apology later after they diagnosed him, which is how I found out about it in the first place, else I would've never known."

"Well, it's good that he reached out to you. Shows he was at least a decent person. Ready for the next question?"

He nods and I ask, "What side of the bed do you prefer?"

He chuckles and side-eyes me. "I suppose the middle isn't an option?"

I laugh and nudge his side with my elbow. "Maybe, if you don't mind a cuddle in the middle of the night."

Ah, there it is, that hint of a blush on his cheeks as he looks down at the gravel path. "I might could get used to that."

"I might could, too."

We both grin as I motion for him to ask the next question. He hums before speaking. "What's your favorite hobby?"

"Oh, that's an easy one. Don't judge me for it but playing video games."

His head whips toward me with a bit of a stunned look in his eyes. "Me too. Geez, we've got a lot in common so far."

I nod. "We sure do."

The entire way back to the cabin, we keep asking more and more questions of each other before agreeing to an early night's sleep. As we head for our rooms, I pause in my doorway and look over at him. "Hey Trevor. One last question."

He stops and raises a brow at me. "Okay."

"Favorite class in an RPG game?"

He chuckles and waggles his brows at me. "Healer, of course. I'm always needed."

I place a hand over my heart and give a dramatic sigh of relief. "Oh good, we won't have to battle it out over choices, and I'll always have someone to keep me alive."

He indulges me with a brief grin of his own. "You're such a dork. I kind of like that."

I can't help but to preen a little at his statement. Score one for me. The boy likes me.

Chapter 11
TREVOR

The bright light of day wakes me earlier than I usually get up at home, making me miss my blackout curtains. I roll groggily from the bed and shove my glasses on my face. After scrubbing my eyes, I make my way to the bathroom to hit the head before wandering into the kitchen, following the scent of fresh coffee. I groan at the sight of a near-full pot. "Bless the morning gods. Please tell me there's sugar and cream in this place."

A husky chuckle sounds from nearby, making me jump. Obviously, he was there. Someone had to make the coffee but my half-dead-still-asleep brain isn't quite online yet. I run a hand through my hair that's no doubt all over my head, like a chia pet's sprouts, and blush clear down to my bare toes. Small miracles I don't sleep nude. A T-shirt with a game controller on it and a pair of black basketball shorts cover my lithe frame from view.

A rumbling voice I could listen read a phonebook accompanies the chuckle. "They stocked the place with whatever you'd probably like to do with your coffee. Flavored cups are in the fridge and there's powder creamer on the counter if you prefer the flavorless shit."

I snicker at his coffee elitism and pull open the fridge, finding they have French vanilla individual cups in a little bin. I grab out two before pulling a mug from the cabinet over the coffee machine. The cabinets have clear glass panes in the light-colored wood for easy searches of what's inside. I add two spoons of sugar in with the creamer before adding fresh coffee.

I let out a moan and close my eyes as the perfection of the life-giving juice hits my tongue in the perfect tones of a well-brewed pot. "Oh, that's so good."

I swear I hear a muffled 'Fucking hell, so damn hot' come from behind me, but when I glance over my shoulder to where Rhodes sits at the island, he's got his phone covering his face. I'm tempted to ask if he said something, but I've never been big on confrontation. I figure if someone said something they want me to know, they'll repeat themselves, so I let it go and take my coffee to the island, climbing onto a stool caddy-corner to his. "Have you been up long?"

He takes the phone from his face and lays it down on the counter before shaking his head. "No, not really. Long enough to wake up, put on the coffee, and drink half a cup. You sleep okay?"

I give him a nod as I drink my coffee. "Yeah, I did. Bed's more comfortable than the one I've got at home."

"Good. I checked the itinerary for today and it says we have our pick of things at the resort before we head to a nearby winery for a late tour and dinner. So, I figure once you're fully coherent, we can go through and pick out some things we can do. I thought we could take turns picking activities."

His words draw a chuckle from me. "You and your plans. Guess it's been working so far, why not? Flip again for first choice?"

He shakes his head. "Nope. You pick first since I asked the first question. Seems fair to me."

I dip my head at him. "What about breakfast? A man can't handle a full day on coffee alone."

Rhodes gives me a warm smile. "We can grab breakfast at the lodge on our way to whatever you pick first. Some activities I saw require giving notice to the front desk staff, so something else to consider."

"Alright. Just one last thing before I think I'm awake enough to handle deciding things. No hiking. I do *not* hike. You hear me?"

Rhodes stares at me for a few seconds before holding his hand out. "As long as you agree we'll finish the day with a nice massage at the spa, we've got a deal."

"Oh, twist my arm, why don't you?"

Note the heavy sarcasm in my tone. *Pfft*. Like I'm going to turn down a chance at free pampering? No thank you, not me. I'm down for that.

I slide my hand into his, feeling a tiny zing of electricity I'd missed the night before as our palms meet. He gives my hand a shake but doesn't immediately release my hand. Instead, he draws it just a smidge closer, as if he wants to drag me to him. To be honest, I'm not sure I would mind if he did.

The moment passes as he relinquishes my hand and

looks down at the folder on the island, which holds all the information on the perks of the resort. He clears his throat and then drains his coffee. He jolts up from his seat and rinses out his cup. "I think I'm going to go grab a shower. We can talk about things over our walk to breakfast."

Before I can get a word out, the man rushes from the kitchen like his ass is on fire. *What the hell was that?*

Chapter 12
RHODES

Holy hell, this entire day is going to wreck me if Trevor keeps on how he's acting, and he's not even doing anything wrong. But the attraction I'm feeling toward him? It's off the freaking charts. From the moans to the adorable, disheveled clothes and hair looking like he'd freshly fucked? I just couldn't handle it anymore. I was glad I'd put on my jeans before leaving my room this morning or he'd have seen just how hard being around him made me.

I didn't have a steel pipe situation on my bingo card for the day, but damn, I'm not sure I've ever felt such a potent attraction to someone else before. Never in my life. Had that man walked into my office over the years while I'd been head down at my work, I'm not sure I'd have been able to ignore him.

I slip into my room to grab some clothes to change into and make my way into the bathroom. With a quick flip of the knob, I get the water heating as I shed my clothes and set them in a pile near the door to take to my room when I'm done.

As steam billows over the top of the shower door, I slide it open and step inside, letting the water rain down upon my skin with a deep sigh. Glancing down at my still hard dick, I know it's going to be a long day if I don't take care of the situation. He just doesn't want to settle down, and I promised Trevor no sexy times for twenty-four hours.

I close my eyes as I wrap my hand around my length, hissing at the first slick stroke of my palm. A vision of what Trevor might look like underneath those clothes floats into my mind and my eyes fly open to stare at the white tile wall. I didn't realize the lust I had for him was so strong, but appears it is.

Normally, a fat cock or a pretty hole are the first things that slip into mind when I'm getting myself off. Not a whole person. It's usually about the orgasm, but as my hand continues to glide along my skin slowly, I can't help but to imagine the source of my desires. God, I want him so fiercely, it's like an ache in my chest...or other areas. I glance down at my hand stroking, and yep, totally aching for something more than it's getting right now, but I'd made a promise.

I force away the image as I place my free hand against the wall and lean on it. Closing my eyes once more, I try to call up an image of myself sliding into a warm, willing body as I tighten my hand, knowing I can't linger in the shower too much longer.

As my hand twists around the head, my mind takes over, providing a lithe body with a pretty dick bobbing between us. *Fuck, it's a glorious sight.* My pace picks up as I watch myself slipping in and out of that body over and over, my hands gripping the trim waist to the point of nearly bruising what's no doubt soft skin.

A hissed *'yes'* falls from my lips as my strokes race along my shaft to the rhythm in my head. My mouth waters to get a taste of the length dancing in the air before it spurts white jets all over the torso of the man beneath me. My grip, both real and imaginary, tightens as the vision expands, showing me a look of pure ecstasy upon Trevor's gorgeous face.

My groan falls loud from my lips before I can stop it as my cock erupts and my orgasm races up and down my spine, white streaking the tiles as it slams into me in rolling waves. I bite my bottom lip to hold back the sound of Trevor's name.

My breathing is heavy and labored as I come down off the high. A solo session has never hit me this hard, and there's only one reason it could be. Trevor. I've only just met the man, and he's already changing so much. I should fear it, but as my cum slowly oozes down the tile wall to the bottom of the tub and down the drain, I find I'm not.

Guilt hits me as I open my eyes, taking in the steamy shower. He hasn't even consented to doing anything with me yet, and I'm already envisioning us together. Whether that's right or wrong, it's not like he'll know. Thing is, I know. All I'm doing is torturing myself should he decide he doesn't want me like that, now or ever. What happens if he finds out the truth of me and the many zeros attached to my name?

The sobering thought has what remains of my interested cock deflating as I climb out of the shower and dry myself off. As the towel soaks up the water droplets from my skin, thoughts whirl around in my brain of both best- and worst-case scenarios of a future with the beautiful Trevor.

If I want him to see me as more than the money in my bank account, I've got to show him more of myself. Show him I'm worth loving before we get to that point. I feel like I've given us a good start so far, showing him it's less about sex for me than the connection we could form with the whole boundary thing, right? Was it far enough, though? Maybe I should make it the entire trip.

I wrinkle my nose up at my reflection in the mirror as I wipe away the fog. No, that's not something I can decide on my own. That part is up to both of us. I won't push him for it. If he makes it noted he wants me, I won't turn him down.

Other than that, all I can do is show him the guy I am beneath the title CEO and the name James Rhodes Williamson, the third. I'll focus on the two of us, and where we are compatible, and go from there. Seems like a solid enough plan.

The guys from the guild like who I am, especially Aravar. Surely Trevor can like me more?

Chapter 13
TREVOR

Okay, so I've only known Rhodes for less than twenty-four hours, but even *I'm* able to tell something's up with him. All throughout breakfast, while he remained the same cordial guy I expect from him, he seemed a bit more reserved. He made no attempts to outright flirt with me, or even make me blush like he had the night before. It's a little unnerving to be honest.

We made some small talk, but mostly we'd focused on making our plans for the day, me getting first pick as he'd mentioned earlier that morning. I wouldn't have held him to it, but I'd gone first. We jammed little activities in, as we wanted to enjoy the winery tonight as well. Thankfully, the no hiking rule I'd put into place had stayed on the table.

The fun of the night before had been missing. I want the teasing Rhodes back. This Rhodes seems like he's just going through the motions of civility to get through the weekend. Sure, if he wanted, he could opt to go home, but who turns down an all-expenses paid trip? Well, I guess for him he'd be getting his money's worth since he did bid for the trip. And while yes, I know the trip was for a date, I wonder sometimes. Am I enough? Am I what he was hoping for?

Somehow, I doubt it. Who wants an extremely introverted, shy virgin who seems scared of his own shadow? That thought makes me frown. Is that why he's changed so much today?

I glance over at him as he mounts the horse the trainers had chosen for him to use for our trail ride this morning as I wait for my turn. I watch the smooth way he swings up into the saddle and the ease he settles himself with. Biting my bottom lip, my mind races with all the little ways we don't match up.

When I'd asked him what he did for work, he'd said he was a businessman, so that already puts him in a different caliber than me. He claims to play video games as a hobby, but that doesn't mean he's as enamored by them as I am. What in the hell can a businessman and a community moderator for an online game really talk about over dinner?

I'm getting ahead of myself as the trainer calls for me to head to the steps to mount up. She'd told me it was the safest way for a less-than-experienced rider to get onto the horse. So, I head for the steps and climb up, swinging my leg over the back of the horse's back and tucking my feet into the stirrups. Out of the corner of my eye, I catch Rhodes watching me and I hope like hell that I look at least somewhat graceful clamoring onto the back of the beast.

It's not like I've never been on a horse before. It might've been ages, but I remember the basics. I shove that thought and all the others away as the trainer leads my horse closer to Rhodes. I give him a small smile as our eyes meet before the trainer's voice catches both of our attentions. "Alright, you two. We've been over the safety protocols, so you both know what to do. Before we hit the trail, we're going to take the horses into the paddock so I can make sure you both have a handle on the basics."

She points to an open doorway to the side of the barn. "One at a time, proceed through those doors."

Since Rhodes is closer and seems to have more recent experience than me, I motion for him to go first, and he turns his dark brown trail horse toward the door. My eyes lock on his broad back as he rocks back and forth in the saddle with the gait of the horse. Everything about the man just does it for me. I didn't realize someone riding a horse could be that sexy but, dang.

I bite my bottom lip as I tear my eyes away and focus in on my mount as it shuffles about, likely having noticed my distraction from the task at hand. I push away any thoughts about Rhodes and his body from my mind, as I'm sure trying to ride a horse with an erection won't be any fun at all. More like torture of the acutest kind.

I give a slight tug to the reins and squeeze my knees to the horse's sides and get the animal moving. So far, so good. It may have been an age and a day since my last riding lesson, but at least I'm remembering the basics.

Sunlight floods me with warmth as we leave the large stable into a white-fenced paddock. The trainer takes the two of us through the paces we'll need to know for the trail ride. As soon as she's satisfied, she leads us out of the paddock toward the trees and a well-defined path between them.

Rhodes offers for me to precede him along the trail, and I shake my head, waving for him to go first. He gives me a curious look before turning his horse to follow the guide. I give mine the lead to follow. As I hit the trail, another employee gets behind me, pulling up the end of our little group. Guess someone responsible for the resort needs to be in back.

As we ride, I look around at the gorgeous scenery surrounding us, but my gaze keeps trailing back to Rhodes and his weird mood since breakfast. I don't know what happened, but whatever it is, I need to fix it. We've only got one night left. While I think I might like to see more of Rhodes after this weekend, I do know I want to lose my v-card to him.

With only one night left of our trip, things need to change. The weird mood needs to go. I stare at his back once more, things playing around in my mind. If this was a video game, what would I do? It's got to be something noticeable. With the way he's been all upfront about sharing things and being transparent, I know subtle hints won't fly.

So far, his plans have worked for us, so now I need to come up with a game plan of my own. Perhaps it's time to channel just a smidge of my best friend. Not become him. *Oh hell, no.* That's got disaster written all over it. Can you see me playing the part of the sassiest little twink you ever saw? No, didn't think so, but even I've got to admit Eliot's got a way with people.

Thoughts of how I act with my friend in the guild when we get flirty flips through my mind, and I twist my tongue in my mouth. Could I do that live and in person? I'll never know if I don't try, and Rhodes? He makes me want to try. I'll start there.

As I put my plan together, I know I need to make it clear to him I'm in this. At least for tonight, but maybe, just maybe, for much longer.

Chapter 14
RHODES

All throughout the trail ride, I would've sworn Trevor's eyes were on me, but every time I turned to look, he only seemed lost in thought. I hope I'm not boring him. Yeah, it's been a while since I've gone on any dates, like since college or whatever, but have I become too work obsessed I can't see the forest through the trees?

As we leave the stables to head to the next activity on our list, canoeing on the lake, I've got to wonder what I was thinking picking that. At least while horseback riding, there's ample space between us. In a boat, the guy's going to be stuck with me in the middle of a lake where all we can do is talk.

I didn't think the whole personal details thing was going to backfire on me like this, but damn, it's hard to hold that stuff back. You don't realize how much of your life includes identifiable details until you're actively trying not to share them.

"You know how to swim, right?"

I kick myself a bit. When we were making plans, I didn't even think to ask. He blinks at me with a weird look on his face. "Of course I can. I wouldn't be going out in a boat with anyone if I couldn't."

Dear brain, it'd be nice if you worked today. I shake my head at his words with a smile. "Of course. Want to get in first?"

He moves into the canoe while I hold it steady until he settles on the seat. As I climb in behind him, he glances over his shoulder at me with a wink. "Ready when you are, captain."

I blink at his playful nature coming out. Oh, today's going to be so much fun.

❤ · ❤ · ❤

Hell. I'm in hell. Pretty sure of that. While I'm trying to play the part of the gentleman and keep myself away from the sexy man life is tempting me to sin with, the shy guy I'd met last night has changed into a little flirt I'm having *so* much trouble turning down. Just want to bend him over a table and have my wicked way with him.

As we leave the lakeside where we'd taken a late lunch picnic to head for the main lodge, I'm left floundering at what to do. This morning, a couple's massage sounded like the perfect idea to relax us before dinner at the Paradise Winery and Vineyard tonight. Now? Hell, as aforementioned. Absolute torture in the fiery depths of Hades. That's what awaits me at the end of this.

As I glance over at the man walking along my side, I steel myself to maintain the boundaries I've put in place. *He's flirty cause he knows it's safe to do so, that's all this is.*

The mantra repeats itself over and over in my head as those brown eyes lift to meet mine. The edges of his soft lips curl up at the start of what I know as the sweetest smile known to mankind. Jesus, what this man does to me. I return it as he speaks. "Ready for a rubdown?"

Somehow, my left foot ends up tangling with my right foot as I take another step and I fall forward, stumbling to right myself as his words overwrite the mantra on repeat. Apparently, his stumbling is contagious because now I'm tripping all over myself because of *his* words.

He laughs while grabbing my arm, aiding in stopping my forward motion. I meet his gaze once more, losing myself to their depths before shaking my head. "Sorry. What'd you ask me?"

An impish look forms upon that beautiful face as he walks off, leaving me where I stand. "I said, are you ready for your massage?"

I scoff, knowing damn well that wasn't what he said, but I'm so not calling him out on it. Let's *not* open that can of worms while I'm helpless to do anything about it or offer any sort of follow through. "Yeah, think I need it after you made me do all that rowing on the lake."

He gives me a wink over his shoulder as I hurry to catch up. "I did offer to help."

"Begrudgingly."

His laugh comes out in soft giggles as he dips his head and watches the ground beneath our feet. "Yeah, well, it was your pick for an activity. Never claimed to be that big of a physical fanatic. Video games are my sport."

"Sadly, the resort doesn't offer video games, or I would've taken you there. Perhaps we should suggest them start an old school arcade here on the comment card before we leave."

He emits a wistful sigh and looks over at me. "Too bad we don't have more time. That would've been lots of fun with you."

I open the lodge doors to let us both in before nodding. "Yeah, it most definitely would be."

The *'maybe after this weekend'* doesn't fall from my lips even though I'm dying to say it. It might be a bit too early to say such things and I promised him no pushing.

We follow the signs leading to the spa and report in for our scheduled time. The room is simple with separate changing stalls. "The door to the right leads into the soaking room. Just head through when you're ready and ring the bell to let staff know to start the timer."

As the employee leaves us in the room to change into the white robes draped over the benches near a row of lockers, I glance over at Trevor, noticing his pink cheeks yet when his eyes meet mine, I see a hint of fear shadowing the depths. Before I can frown or question anything, he drops his eyes to scoop up the attire. As he steps into a stall, he glances back at me. "Just in case I forget to tell you later, I've had an amazing time."

He turns away, leaving me staring after him with a smile beaming on my face. Perhaps I'm not wrong. Maybe after this weekend will happen.

♥·♥·♥

Did I say I was in hell earlier? I was wrong. *So* fucking dead wrong. I did *not* know when I signed up for the couple's massage that it would include an aromatherapy soak beforehand. As the white terry cloth slips from Trevor's shoulders, exposing the pristine skin of his slender back, my mouth waters, wanting to taste and lick every inch of that exposed flesh.

The spa had given us little black boxer style shorts without the front slit to wear in place of our clothes, and his hugs a supple ass with just the right amount of jiggle to it, sending my thoughts careening back to my jerk off session in the shower this morning. By the gods, my imagination wasn't too far off.

I bite down on my bottom lip to hold in my whimpers as he sinks down in one of the two side-by-side tubs with a heavenly sigh. Unconsciously, I take a step forward, my right hand lifting as if to reach out and run itself along the water-slicked skin. Trevor rests his head against the pillow and looks over at me with a quirked brow. "You going to get in? The water's nice."

His words bring me back to the present and I turn away, allowing my robe to drop to the bench before I quickly sink into my bath, concealing the stiffness these boxers in no way hide beneath the surface of the bubbling water. I let out a sigh, perhaps not just from how relaxing it feels, and rest against the pillow.

I send up a tiny prayer for patience and help to get my starving libido under control before I turn my head toward him with a slight smile. "Still okay with this? I thought it was just the massage."

His answering smile reassures me as he shrugs. "Sometimes we all need the unexpected, don't you think?"

I nod, because hell, he was unexpected and I'm suspecting I damn well need him.

Chapter 15
TREVOR

Having to dress down in front of someone else hadn't occurred to me until I'd seen the robe and tiny black shorts sitting on the bench. So many thoughts had run through my head at the sight of them, from fear of not being ready for such a step to the naughty, naughty things the sexy Rhodes could do to me. It's fifty-fifty, really. They say love and hate are a fine line, but so are fear and lust. You can want something so fiercely, but fear reaching for it.

Still being in the second camp, I'd retreated to the changing stall rather than bare it all right before his beautiful blue eyes. I'd need to get over that if I want the man to sex me up before the weekend is over, but those thoughts could wait. I'd forced away the fear and sank into the bath with Rhodes in the one next to me.

So far, so good. I'd made it into the tub, and now I stare up at the gorgeous body of the man who'd bid on me. The pale skin stretches over taut lines of muscles of someone who looks out for themselves, but probably doesn't see a lot of sunlight. I can't fault the man for the last. I'm not a huge fan of a lot of sunlight myself, as evidenced by the light hue of my flesh.

It all disappears under the surface of the water in the tub next to mine until all either of us can see of the other are our heads. I turn to face him, gracing him with another sweet smile as the heat unfurls all the tightness in my muscles from all the anxiety which had built up for this weekend. I take a deep inhale, letting the scents of lavender and sage work their magic on my senses.

Rhodes hums and turns his head to face me as well. "You were almost right. Feels a bit like heaven right now."

I chuckle softly and swirl my fingers around in the water absentmindedly, unable to sit still even in such a relaxing space. No doubt it'll take nearly the entire session to work out all the kinks and knots my anxiety wrought. "Heaven isn't nice?"

"Well, it's a step up from nice, if others are to be believed."

I suppose he has a point if he's talking about the kind people believe is a cloud city with roads paved with gold. Sounds gaudy to me, but hey, what do I really know about such a place? It's not like the people who raised me took me to any sort of faith-based places, or any place really.

Banishing thoughts of my past, I focus on Rhodes, on this moment right here. "Depends on what you think heaven is."

"What do you think it is?"

I entwine my fingers and look down at the water, lost in thought. "Hmm. Not so sure if it exists, to be honest, but if I were to define my own personal heaven? I'd say it happens during life, not after death."

His body shifts, as if he's turning more of his body to face me, drawing my gaze from the water back to him. "Why do you say that?"

I give his words more thought before twisting my body like he did. "Well, why should we have to die to experience something like that? Life is crappy enough as it is. Shouldn't we have something to look forward to now?"

"Some might say it's our reward for making it through life."

I shrug at his words. "Perhaps, but that could be a really long wait for some people. Why should we wait and see what someone else has defined heaven as when we can determine our own long before then?"

Rhodes turns his gaze toward the ceiling and silence fills the space between us, only broken by the soft laps of water against the sides of the tubs. Mood music still plays softly in the background, but it's not loud enough to detract from any conversations lovers might have. Or two people with the potential to be lovers.

After a few moments, Rhodes finally speaks. "I've never thought about things that way. You've got a rather good point. Leads back to my original question, but perhaps I should reframe it. What is your heaven?"

I chuckle and look up at the ceiling. "Oh, that's an easy one to answer. All the games I love to play and being surrounded by the ones I love to play those games with. It's simple, really. Having my chosen family around me just doing what we love so much. It's perfection."

He sighs and I look over at him to see if he thought

my answer's stupid, but he has a wistful smile upon his face. He turns to meet my gaze. "That does sound like heaven. I'd want to share such a place with you."

His words bring a smile to my face. "Yeah? I know you said you enjoyed playing video games, but I wasn't sure if you were a casual gamer or what."

He chuckles and raises a hand out of the water to rest it on the side of the tub. "Definitely not a casual gamer, but I do have to break up my gaming time with that thing people call work. While some of it isn't my favorite, and without telling you where I work or what I specifically do, there are parts of my career I absolutely love. Seeing the reactions my work brings to people is life-changing for me."

"I can't say I know what that's like. I deal with angry and frustrated people. Not very rewarding, but it pays the bills and keeps me in my video games, so for now, it works. Maybe one day."

I may be a community moderator for my all-time favorite game, but it's still a customer service role, and those always suck. I'm hoping to save up enough to go to school and get my developer's certification, but I'm not there yet.

"If it's something you want, I'm sure you'll get there."

I perk a brow at his words. "How are you so sure? I'm usually a mess and a big 'fraidy cat. You saw me when we first met outside the lodge, remember?"

He chuckles and nods his head. "Oh yeah, I remember. I've also had a front-row seat to watching you step outside your comfort zone all weekend. If you can do this, you can do anything else you put your mind to."

I blink at him, mouth hanging open before I shut it, blushing clear to the tips of my toes, and I look down at the water again. If someone as polished as Rhodes believes in me so much, why can't I put as much faith in myself?

A soft chime sounds in the room before I come up with an answer for either him or myself and the attendant enters the room. She passes us each a towel and gives us our instructions before leading us to the next room, where two padded beds await.

I still don't know what the heck to say to Rhodes.

Chapter 16
RHODES

Even though we'd toweled off before leaving the bathing room, we were still in our damp shorts. I open my mouth to ask about that when the attendant hands each of us a sheet and points to a screen. The briefs are to be left in a hamper there and we're to wrap up in the sheet and get on the beds, face down.

She leaves us alone and I motion to the screen. "You go first."

Trevor disappears behind the screen, but I watch him as he goes, my eyes dropping to the tiny black shorts hugging the round globes of his ass. I bite my bottom lip and look down at my dick twitching in my own tiny shorts. I glare at it and give it silent instructions to stay down. This isn't the type of massage with a happy ending, at least, not right now, at any rate.

Perhaps that's my cock brain being hopeful *something* will happen this weekend, but the man is so fucking hot it's difficult not to be eternally hopeful. Trevor's voice summons me from my silent conversation with my privates, and I look up to see him standing by the beds. "Your turn."

I guess I was so lost in thoughts of how hot he is I missed him coming out from behind the screen. I nod and disappear behind it. As my dick flops free of the shorts, I groan at how chubby it's looking right now. I can't think about how sexy he is, or Mr. Happy is going to keep getting happier.

I turn my attention to removing the cold, wet shorts and dumping them into the hamper with the others and drying off any remaining water. I dump the towel into another bin marked for them and wrap the sheet around my waist. With a couple of deep breaths to steady myself, I round the screen to find Trevor's hopped up onto the table and is sitting there, swinging his feet.

His gaze raises up to mine with a shy smile, one I can't help but return as I walk over to stand before him, gazing into his eyes to see if any of the fear remains from earlier. I see none and I'm grateful for that. "Ready for total relaxation?"

He chuckles. "I don't even know what that feels like, but bring it on."

He keeps making brief comments like that, making me wonder what sort of life he leads. It's like a puzzle and I'm not only missing some major pieces, but I don't have the picture on the box anymore either. We'll get there, if fate wills it, and damn, I hope she does. Already, even with what little I truly know, the man is getting under my skin, and not just sexually.

I reach up and brush a wayward lock of hair from

his face, grazing his forehead with the tips of my fingers. "You're in for a treat, then. A place like this is bound to have good staff."

"I hope so. I've heard about people who get these on the reg and seem to enjoy them. Bet something like that would be nice."

"No doubt it is. I know when I have gotten some in the past because my muscles were too tight, I always felt like a mess of jello afterwards."

His nose wrinkles up all cute-like, making my fingers twitch with the urge to tweak it, but I refrain. "That doesn't sound too appealing."

I laugh and shake my head. With a wicked grin, I lean in to whisper low in his ear, "It's like being pounded into the mattress and coming so hard you lose sense of the universe."

Was that a whimper I heard? I stand back up and a pair of glassy eyes stare up at me, pink lips parted as if inviting me to delve between them and get my first taste of this delightful man sitting so temptingly before me. So much for keeping my cock deflated cause I just shot both of us into the stratosphere. At least now I have an answer to a question I'd not dared even ask my inner self. He wants me.

Screw waiting. I need a taste. I lean in, mere inches from that pair of soft lips, when a knock comes from the door, bringing me back to my senses. I stumble back a step or two before the door opens and I'm grateful the shock sent my dick back down.

I glance over my shoulder to see two staff members enter the room, smiling at us. "Hey guys. Ready for your massage?"

I nod and Trevor lets out a choked laugh, his hands covering up his groin. Guess the shock didn't help him out as much as it did me. I doubt we're the first people to get hard during a couple's massage. Probably not going to be the last either.

I move over to the other table and hop up on it like Trevor's sitting as one attendant grabs some oil from the warmers on the counter and other implements they might need while the other approaches the beds. "I'm Georgia and this is Brenna. We'll be your masseuses today. We're going to start with your backs, so I'll need you to lie down on your fronts with your face in the ring. So, get situated and we'll get started."

As we both re-situate ourselves upon the beds as directed, she walks over to the wall and pokes at a little screen embedded there. Soothing sounds of the rainforest or the ocean or something like that play over the speakers in the ceiling, along with the soft tinkle of the most melodic wind chimes I've ever heard. It's quite soothing and I feel myself relaxing even more than the hot soak had done.

I glance over to Trevor and see Brenna has stepped up next to him as he lays with his head in the ring, so I set my head into mine. One woman speaks again, "Alright guys, just relax and enjoy. Talk to each other and pretend we're not here."

I guess they didn't need our confirmation to any of that as hands covered with warm oil come down on my skin and knead the muscles of my shoulders. I close my eyes and sink into the cushioning beneath me. The woman has a soft but firm touch, perfect in the way I like, as if the woman's worked on me before.

"Wow, that already feels so amazing."

Trevor's voice comes from beside me, making me laugh. "It's going to feel even more amazing. Just you wait."

They'd placed the two tables side-by-side and I feel fingers clutch mine before Trevor speaks. "This was a great idea. Thanks for bringing me here."

"You're most welcome."

For a while, we both go silent, simply enjoying the massage as the two women work their magic upon our muscles. I hate I didn't get to see what response Trevor would've had to my comment about being pounded, but maybe that's not such a bad thing. The look of glazed lust on his face and in his deep brown eyes had grabbed me by the balls, making me salivate for more than just a little taste of him.

Trevor groans, low and deep, at something the masseuse does to him, his voice following it up. "Okay. Heaven just changed."

I'm tempted to lift my head and see what's being done to him, but I keep my relaxed pose as my masseuse works on the knots at my shoulder blades from all the hunching over my desk I've been doing for weeks. "Why do you say that?"

"I need to add a masseuse to heaven. This is a must-have for any dream existence."

I chuckle softly and squeeze the hand still holding

mine. "That's a good plan."

He's right though. Heaven *did* just change. I want him to be a huge part of mine.

Chapter 17
TREVOR

After experiencing heaven as my first ever massage, it was time to head for the winery for our tour and dinner. Even with the full day we've had so far, I'm feeling energized to face the rest of the evening to come.

As I slide into the back of the town car waiting for us, I sigh as my already relaxed body sinks into the plush leather seat. I don't know if I've ever been this relaxed around another person, and it's not just the massage either. Every step of the way, Rhodes has taken care of me, making sure I feel safe in whatever space we're in. He doesn't know it, but that's meant the absolute world to me.

I feel like he's someone I can trust. As I glance over at his handsome face as he climbs into the car beside me, I make another plan of my own. Tonight will be about opening up a little more. Don't need to share too many identifying details to shed a little more light on what makes me who I am. Perhaps it'll help him understand me even more than he appears to.

He gives me a warm smile as we both buckle in before the driver sets off on a smooth pace through the tree-lined road, taking us away from the resort for our jaunt to the winery.

This weekend has been one of the most, if not the most, amazing of my still-young life. I know for sure it's going to go down in the history books for me. Perhaps Eliot wasn't wrong when he suggested this trip. While Rhodes is probably not my forever man, he could be Mr. Right-First-Time. I'd place a bet he'd take good care of me, especially if I told him I was a virgin.

It's not like I can't tell he's interested in me like that. The heat in his gaze has been searing me all day, and the way his eyes slowly traveled along my near-naked body during our couple's massage? It was almost enough to have me drop those little spa shorts right then and there to beg the sexy man to have his way with me, but I'm not quite bold enough for that.

Before the dirty thoughts take over my mental faculties yet again today, I force them away to focus in on the more important, the here-and-now, on Rhodes. "So, how much of a paradise do you think this winery is?"

With a chuckle, Rhodes twists his body in the seat a bit, so he's facing me. I do the same, so neither of us has to crook our necks to talk. "Hoping for a little happy ending?"

My gaze drops to my lap as I feel a blush coming over me but give a little shrug of my shoulders. "Maybe. Couldn't hurt to hope, right?"

"Not at all."

Our gazes meet and we both grin. Conscious of the driver in the front seat, I turn the topic to safer things than the alluded to happy endings for the rest of the drive to the winery and throughout the tour once we get there.

❤ · ❤ · ❤

As we'd arrived at the winery, a tour had been about to leave, so someone had quickly directed us to join them. It had been gorgeous seeing all the vines laid out, had been interesting learning about the different varietals and the methods the winery uses. I never knew so much went into a place like this.

Our table was ready by the time the tour and tasting session were over, so they seated us straight away. We chatted until the server took our orders. As the server stepped away from our table, a man approaches us with a smile of pure customer service spread across his face.

The guy's black shirt clearly spells out that he works here and, according to his nametag, he's Mateo Cruz. He's hot, with his broad height, tanned skin, and dark hair, but nowhere near as sexy as Rhodes is. His tattoo sleeves catch my attention and I try to pick out the pattern, but he speaks, garnering my attention back to his face.

"Good evening, gentleman. I just wanted to stop by the table and check in with you guys. I'm the manager here at Paradise Winery and if you guys need anything, ask for me. My name's Mateo Cruz. Is there anything I can help you with at the moment?"

I shake my head and glance over at Rhodes. He gives the manager a smile. "I think we're good so far. It's a gorgeous place you have here, Mr. Cruz."

Mateo's customer service smile turns into a genuine one and he dips his head into a nod. "We appreciate that. I'll leave you guys to enjoy your dinner and hope we'll see you with us again in the future. Have a good night!"

We both say our goodbyes and Mateo leaves us alone to the seclusion of our table. I chuckle softly as my eyes meet Rhodes'. "Well, you've got to hand it to this place. They know how to make people feel special. Just like you."

Rhodes' glass halts halfway to his lips before he sets it down, letting his hand come to rest upon the table between us. "You're worth treating special."

I swallow and drop my gaze to his hand. "Aside from my best friend, it's been a really long time since anyone thought I was anything close to special."

Rhodes frowns and leans toward the table more, his gaze intent upon me even though I'm not looking up at him. "Why do you say that? I don't see how that's true. What about your parents?"

Few people think about stories like mine right off hand. To some, it seems to shock them into remembering not everyone's life is picture perfect, like the movies show all the time. I force myself to meet his gaze. "They died when I was seven in a car accident. The only family they could find to take me in turned out to be a heroin junkie who tried to sell me for a hit."

Talk about dropping a bomb in the middle of the table, but I need Rhodes to know all this, to let him make an informed decision about if I'm really something he wants in his life. I don't see how he could, but at least I'm offering him the chance to decide on his own.

He stares at me, features contorted into a visage of horror at the simple way I'd shared my history. It's easy to imagine what sort of images are going through his head right now, stories of child trafficking, no doubt. It would've been so easy for me to become just another statistic. His mouth opens and closes a few times before he sinks back against his seat, Adam's apple bobbing with a very visible swallow. "I'm so sorry. What…? No, I won't press you to tell me more and bring back up any traumatic memories."

I'm truly touched by his consideration. There's been so many who found themselves horribly fascinated by a potential tale of misery and woe. They pressed me for my story, to make me spill it all. Him though? I want him to know. Heck, I need him to know this about me. "It's not as bad as your mind is probably making it. I barely remember it all, but I guess you could call me one of the lucky ones."

His frown deepens. "How can anyone be lucky in a situation like that?"

I sip from the water glass. I'd had enough wine during the tasting for the evening. "Because the dealer my uncle tried selling me to thankfully had a conscience. Sure, drugs might be bad, but selling a child? Especially for drugs? To him, that was as evil as you could get. The guy put in an anonymous call to CPS and dropped me off at the emergency room. I ended up in the system until I aged out at eighteen. Aside from a lot of being ignored by people just doing it to get a check, I never ended up in a house with abusers."

A wry chuckle falls from my lips, and I look down at

my lap where I've draped my napkin and am now wringing it in my hands, nervous about how Rhodes will react to my complete story. "I always chalked it up to my parents watching over me all these years, keeping me safe the only way they could."

"Oh, Trevor."

Rhodes lets out a heavy sigh, and I catch his head shaking as he stares over at me. Yep, this is it. I just killed anything we could've had before it even started.

Chapter 18
RHODES

What the hell do you say to all that? I'm sorry just doesn't seem to cut it. Sure, it's not as bad as some of the horror stories I've heard, but hell, losing his parents is sad enough all on its own without the rest. Every instinct I possess has me wanting to crawl over the table and wrap him up in myself to keep him safe for the rest of his life.

Fighting my body's drive, I drop my gaze to the table as I try to come up with something, anything, to say to him. No doubt my silence is making him antsy, but my mind is completely failing me. I've always known what to say in awkward situations. Growing up as the heir of my family, they'd drilled social constructs into me, but even that didn't cover situations such as we're in.

"It's cool, Rhodes. We can ignore everything I've said and just keep things light and upbeat the rest of the weekend if you want to."

My head jerks up and my eyes widen as I stare across

the table at him. What the fuck? No longer able to constrain myself to my seat, I get up, drawing Trevor's eyes back to me as I come around the table and sink down into a crouch beside his chair. I reach out to take his hand and draw it to my lips for a soft kiss. "Sweetheart, no. There's nothing to ignore. Your story is a part of what makes you who you are, and I want to know these things about you. That's not what keeps me quiet."

The endearment falls so easily from my lips, and I don't regret it. He studies my eyes and I hope my sincerity shows in my gaze. "Then why?"

I give a soft sigh and let my thumb rub along his knuckles, the slightly dry skin rough against the pad of my finger. "I don't want to spout off all the platitudes I know you've heard before. It blows me away that you feel safe enough to trust me with your history. So much since we met makes sense, so the fact you're trusting me with this? I'm touched by it."

A dubious look crosses his features as he stares at me. "Are you serious?"

I nod my head vigorously. "Of course I am."

"Most people do what you said, offer insincere words and shove me to the back of their minds once I'm not in their faces."

I turn his hand over and lean in to place a gentle kiss on his palm before meeting his steady gaze. "I promise you, I have no desire to do that. Never with you. I'm looking forward to learning more about you, happy, sad, or otherwise. Hopeful for that, at any rate, if it's something you'll want at the end of the trip."

My words bring a hopeful glint to his brown eyes,

making a fire well up inside me to see that it's something that happens when we go back home. I've put so much time and effort into my company all these years, no doubt I'm able to do the same with a relationship.

His next words reflect the look in his eyes. "You think you'll want that? What if we don't even live in the same city, or heck, the same state?"

I chuckle as I unfold myself from the crouch as my knees ache a bit from holding the position for so long. I let his hand drop from mine as I cross back around the table to sink into my seat and meet his gaze once more. "We'll work at it, figure out how things work best for us. If we decide before we go home we want this, we'll communicate and talk things through. Stuff worth having is worth working hard for, don't you think?"

His head bobs up and down. "Definitely. I just... I've never felt the whole silver platter situation people talk about, yet this whole opportunity with you feels like it's served on a gold one. It's kind of hard to trust that it won't get yanked away from me, you know what I mean?"

The urge to wrinkle my nose at his wording, considering I was born with a golden spoon in my mouth, is hard to fight. I don't want to just come out and say that I don't really understand what that's like, but if I take it from a standpoint of risk management, I get it. "The more you stand to gain, the more you risk. It's a gigantic leap of faith to make, but how about instead of making that leap now? Let's do so at the end of the weekend. That way we can enjoy the rest of our stay without the will-he-or-won't-he hanging over our heads."

"You always have such good plans?"

I can't help but chuckle and wink at his words. "If you want to think that. Sometimes, it's just damn good luck."

His foot bumps against mine under the table as he laughs softly with a shake of his head, sending his dark hair to dance on his head. "I'll take a bit of that luck."

"I'm more than willing to share it with you."

The server approaches the table, bringing our conversation to a pause as they pour out two glasses of the wine we'd order and then places our food before us, sending divine aromas into the air and making me salivate for more than just a taste of the man across from me.

"Enjoy your meal, guys. Let me know if I can get you anything else."

We're left in peace again and we both dig into our meals. No doubt the day's activities made him as ravenous as they'd made me. Working in the office, I rarely get that much physical activity in a day. I pick up my wineglass and hold it out toward him. "Here's to the rest of an amazing weekend."

He picks up his own glass and the two meet with a soft clink as he smiles. "Cheers to that."

I send up a silent prayer to whoever might be listening in the universe. *Please let him be the one for me.*

Chapter 19
TREVOR

This has got to be a dream, right? Life hasn't seriously just handed me not only the most amazing weekend with the best food I've ever had in my life, but also a man worth his weight in solid gold. Stuff like this doesn't happen to me, it just doesn't.

I take a sip of my wine, so tempted to drain the thing in one gulp and make me have a rosy-glasses type of situation for the rest of the night, but I refrain. If this isn't a dream, I want to remember it when it's all over and done with. Not to mention that if I want sexy times to happen, I'm probably not going to get that if I'm all sloshy and even a hint of too far past buzzed to be considered.

I set the glass down and focus on the food, taking a few bites before I let my gaze travel back to Rhodes. "Since you're the man with all the plans. When do we share more personal details? Tomorrow before we leave, or are we going to trade numbers and where we live and handle the rest when we get home?"

As he chews, he looks like he's lost in thought for a moment. Guess the man with all the plans doesn't have all the answers right out of the gate. Good to see he's not the superhuman man-computer I was believing he could be.

"Well, hard to say since we've not decided on after the weekend. Suppose we'll play it by ear and make that decision then, too."

I nod, and he speaks again. "There is one more activity I'd like to do tonight before we go to sleep, if you're game."

I quirk a brow at his words and roll my hand toward him. "What's that?"

"Take advantage of the decking of the treehouse to stargaze? I live in a city so I don't get a lot of time where it's dark enough to see stars like we can see here. I'd love to share that with you."

He actually blushes at the admission and looks down at his plate as if worried I'd refuse him. Like I could. His words briefly remind me of StarGazer, and I hope he's having a good weekend. The pang doesn't hit as hard as it had in previous times, perhaps because I'm really coming to like Rhodes and want to spend more time with him. So, I nod. "I'd love that. It sounds like fun. You'll point things out to me?"

He chuckles softly and lifts his head to meet my eyes, a twinkle dancing within the depths. "As long as you promise to sit with me."

"Is that so?"

He nods. "Absolutely. It's so much easier to point things out if you can look directly down my fingertip."

I can't help the laugh that spills from me at his attempt to convince me to let him hold me. I slide my hand across the table and hold his this time. "As long as you plan to cuddle me close, you've got a deal."

He turns his hand to thread his fingers with mine and holds to it, never looking away from my eyes. "I'll hold you all night long if you'll let me."

His words make my heart beat faster and my breathing hitches. No one had uttered those words to me before and in this moment, I treasure them more than any I've heard from him so far, even when he felt honored about me trusting him. All I've ever wanted is someone to keep me safe, to hold me tight. Right here and now, he's offering that to me, at least for a night. I'd be a dumbass to turn that down. "All night."

He grins. "Let's get finished here, shall we?"

His *'shall we'* makes me snicker and I take a sip of the wine. "Very well. We shall, my good man."

I give him a wink before digging into my food. With a laugh, he nudges my foot with a warm smile. "Oh, you hush."

I mock gasp and lay my left hand over my heart as if I'm wounded. "Me, sir? How have I offended you so?"

I can't hold back the giggle at my horrendous play-acting, and he joins me. His hand slides across the table and takes hold of mine to give it a squeeze. "Absolutely nothing. I hope you're having a wonderful trip so far."

My giggle taper off and I give him a genuine smile I feel all the way down to my toes. "It's one of the best."

"Good."

We tuck into our food, making small talk for the rest

of the meal, whether we're dog or cat people—both dog people, for your information—and other random topics. Before too long, we're done eating and make our way outside into the night.

He holds his arm out to me. "How about a walk around the front of the grounds while we wait for the car to arrive?"

I slide my arm through his and lean against him, seeking comfort in the warmth emanating from him. "Lead the way, sir."

He chuckles and we walk, taking in the sights while waiting for the car, and for me, the rest of the night to come.

❤·❤·❤

I rest my cheek on my arms on the countertop as he fetches me a bottle of water from the fridge. Aside from the tasting, I'd only had the one glass of wine with our dinner, but it had given me cotton mouth. He sets it down next to my arm. "Here you go, sweetheart."

He leans in toward me and as I turn my head to thank him, our lips meet for one second, then two. My lips tingle with the contact and the breath stills in my lungs. Oh my heavens, Rhodes and I are kissing. I've never felt such electricity, such a connection in the brief experiences I've had with kissing in the past.

With a gasp, Rhodes takes a slight step back as he yanks himself from me. He stares at me a moment before stammering, "Sorr..."

Before the words of apology fully leave his tongue, I slip from my seat and reach up for the back of his head, yanking his mouth back to mine. Our lips smash together and I kiss him again. This time, Rhodes stands in shock, not returning my kiss until I press the full length of my body against his, spurring him into action.

His tongue swipes along my bottom lip, nudging the small space between them before I open for him, letting him inside to taste me. I suck on his tongue as it delves inside my mouth, drawing a groan from him as his arms wrap around my waist like iron bands, clasping my body hard against his.

I slide my other arm up and wrap both around his neck, rising onto my toes to press harder into the kiss, as lost to the desire and sensation as he is. Our tongues swap and I get my first taste of him, red wine mixed with mint and a unique flavor I know only as his.

A whimper leaves the back of my throat as he pulls back from the kiss, both of us drawing in large lungfuls of air. Rhodes places his forehead against mine and shuts his eyes for a moment, looking like he's trying to compose himself. I tilt my head to press another kiss to his lips and he groans again, this time sounding both mega turned on but also a bit frustrated. "Trevor, we need to..."

I press my lips to his again, and he allows this one. We don't need to do any more thinking or talking. I know what I'm doing. I know what I want. What I want, is him.

Chapter 20
RHODES

Magnificent. How can something feel so right? I don't want to doubt what's going on between us, but I've made promises to him, promises I need to keep. If I break my word now and he regrets anything happening between us, he'll have no reason to trust me in the future.

Steeling my resolve, I pull back from our kiss yet again, and this time, push him away from me a bit, gaining some sort of space between our hard bodies. His adorable face pouts up at me, his eyes reflecting his frustration with me pulling away like I keep doing. "Don't you want me, Rhodes?"

His question rips a hole open inside me. How can he ask me that with how I'm responding to him? I lift a hand to curl it around the side of his face, allowing my thumb to brush along the apple of his cheek. "Oh sweetheart, of course I do. So fucking much, I ache with it."

He frowns. "Then why do you keep stopping?"

"I promised you I wouldn't push you on this."

He rolls his eyes so hard I'm sure the astronauts on the space station could've seen it. "Christ, Rhodes. I may be a virgin, but I'm not some blushing noob who doesn't know how a dick works."

For a moment, I stare at him. I'm pretty sure I'm supposed to tell him he needs to save his first time for someone special, but damnit, I want him too much for that. I can make this special for him, a night he'll remember for the many years of his life to come. God, how I want to be that guy for him. Without a second thought, I go for it. "I need the words, Trevor. Tell me you want this, that you want me, and I'll take you to my bed and not stop until I'm buried deep inside you."

At my words, he presses back into my arms, forcing my hand to fall away from his cheek. He tightens his grip around my neck and wraps one leg around my hip before hopping up and latching on with the other. In instinct, I grab hold of his ass cheeks, holding him tight as he climbs me like a tree. He meets my gaze head-on. "Make me yours, Rhodes."

As his hardness presses against my own, I groan and grip his ass as I head toward the bedroom. "With pleasure."

I take hold of his mouth again, thrusting my tongue inside his mouth as he parts his lips like I want to be thrusting into his body. Oh hell, his taste. I can't get enough of it.

We bump into a wall, and I press him into it, unwilling to tear my mouth away to find the doorway. He wiggles in my arms, and I grind myself into him, drawing the sweetest whimper from the back of his throat. His fingers dig into my hair, and he yanks my head back. I meet his eyes, wild and unfocused from the lust and want coursing through his veins. A plea falls from his lips in the husky tone of a man being pushed to the brink. "Please Rhodes, naked. I want to see you."

A vision of him naked underneath me slams into my brain from my jerk-off session and I growl a bit and lean in to place a kiss where his neck meets his shoulder. I pull us from the wall and rush into the bedroom. His feet swing from around my hips to the floor with a thud and he reaches for the buttons on my shirt. I take his hands to stop him. He groans and looks up at my face. "No more stopping."

I shake my head at his words. "Not stopping. Stripping. For you."

I give him a gentle push and he sinks down onto the edge of the bed, sitting there staring up at me, waiting. I trail my fingers up my chest along the seam of the shirt, toying with the buttons, yet not undoing them. His eyes follow my fingers, tongue sliding along his lips as if anticipating what's coming.

I slip the first button free, then the next, slowly working my way down. As the shirt gapes open, he looks a smidge disappointed at the view, but I can't blame him for that. Instead of the bare skin he was no doubt hoping for, all he sees is my white undershirt. I chuckle softly and reach to undo my cuffs. "Something wrong?"

His eyes bounce between the movement of my hands and my eyes. "Other than the white t-shirt I want to rip from your body with my bare hands?"

I drop my hands to my sides, letting my dress shirt

slide from my arms to fall to the floor. After freeing myself from the cloth, I dance my fingers along my abs over the shirt in question. "Ah, but you've seen what's beneath this shirt."

He swallows and reaches out to run his fingers along the zip of my pants where my stiff shaft hides as he stares straight into my eyes. "But I haven't seen this."

His touch, gentle as it is, draws a shudder from me and I curse my idea of stripping down seductively for him, at the thought of taking this slow. *First time, first time, first time.* The refrain echoes in my mind like a litany. I keep myself from pouncing on him like a jungle cat on its prey and give him a wicked smile. Grasping his hand, I press it against my covered cock, letting him feel exactly how hard he's made me. "Oh, trust me, sweetheart, it'll be worth the wait."

His fingers curl around me and give me a little tug, making me gasp at the sensation as another thread of want unfurls within me. I lean down and capture his lips with mine before standing up and whipping the shirt over my head and tossing it to the side. Maybe we're both right. A little faster won't hurt.

He grins as if he's won the battle and reaches for my pant's clasp. I grab his hands and pull them away with a soft *'tsk tsk'*. "Nope. Sit back and watch, sweetheart."

He huffs and then reaches for the hem of his own shirt. Before I'm able to stop him, he's whipped the polo over his head, sending his dark mess of hair into several directions. As I take in his pebbled nipples on what looks like the smoothest flesh with just a hint of hair, I know I've lost. With a growl, I pull at the button of my pants and nod to him. "Get naked and in the middle of the bed."

For a man who came off so shy earlier, he's seemed to have lost it by now. His clothes are gone in what seems like the blink of an eye and he splays out in the center of the bed like a prince, cock jutting up proudly from a nest of hair as dark as the sky outside. Oh yeah, I'm gonna make that man mine.

I shove my pants and underwear down with no ceremony and shove my way out of everything with my feet, shoes included. I prowl up the bed between his legs and prop myself up on one hand next to his shoulder. My eyes trail down along his neck to his chest, fingers following along the path as an unbidden whisper is pulled from me. "God, but you are beautiful, aren't you?"

His skin pebbles in the wake of my touch and I lean down to take one of the hardened nubs into my mouth, sucking on the bud and drawing the sweetest cries from the sweetest man I've ever had in my bed, or hell, maybe even in my life.

Chapter 21
TREVOR

Mother trucking shizballs. His mouth's on me. I've got a man's freaking mouth on me. I've been waiting for this day for so long, I'd lamented it would ever happen. The warm, wet touch of his tongue against my nipple makes me arch up into his mouth as if my body's begging for more.

My eyes drift shut, and I thrust my hands into his hair, letting the cool strands filter through my fingers as I clutch to him. He switches to the other side of my chest, giving that nipple the same glorious attention as the first. Perhaps I was wrong about heaven. Heaven might very well be in this man's bed, his touch electrifying all my senses and awakening my body in ways I never knew existed.

He trails kisses and soft nips along my skin, leading downward, making me ease my grip on his head so he can keep exploring me. As he reaches my navel, his chin bumps my dick, the coarse scruff abrading the soft skin. I draw in a quick breath, hoping and freaking praying the man puts his mouth on me.

I open my eyes and tilt my head down because I don't want to miss a moment of this show. Rhodes' eyes are on me as he opens his mouth and his tongue slips out, sliding along my slit. I let out the breath I'd taken in a whoosh with a moan. "Oh god."

As he traps the head of my cut cock in the warm cavern of his mouth, my eyes nearly roll out of the back of my head at the sensation. I've never felt anything so deliciously sinful in my life as this man's mouth. He swirls his tongue around the tip before sliding his lips along the shaft and sucking on me.

I groan long and low as my hips thrust up. He presses down on them, pinning me in place on the bed as he bathes my shaft with his attentions, his soft hums and moans vibrating along my skin. I might've never had another man's mouth on me before, but holy Hades, he's got to have one of the best.

He drapes an arm over my abs to hold me in place while the free one wraps around my shaft. As he adds stroking to the sucking, my fingers clutch at the bedsheets, fingernails scrabbling for purchase on the fabric, so I don't grab his head and shove him all the way down on my dick.

It isn't but a few minutes of his attention and he has me wriggling beneath him, helpless whimpers coming from me as I try hard not to shoot off in his mouth already. "Oh god, you need to stop. *Stop*. I don't want to come yet. Don't want this to be over. *Oh god*."

He pulls off me with a pop and lets out a dark chuckle. "Oh sweetheart, you'll get hard for me again, I promise. We've got all night long."

He dives back down on me again, taking me into the back of his throat with a swallow. My balls tighten and I cry out as my first orgasm with another man rips through me, rolling along my skin with each spurt of my cum as it jets into his mouth. As the world whites out around me, I

♥·♥·♥

lose track of reality as I wallow in the bliss.
I come back to awareness with soft kisses and nose nuzzles against the side of my face while Rhodes whispers sweet little nothings into my ear. "You taste so sweet, baby."

I turn my face into the kisses, and our lips meet. Sliding my arms around his neck and holding him close, both of us trade lazy kisses while his still-hard dick presses into my hip. I hum low as he pulls back. "That was so good."

He chuckles softly and places a kiss on my nose. "Glad you enjoyed it."

I open my eyes to look up at him, meeting his steady ones as his fingers brush the opposite cheek he'd been nuzzling. "Coming back to me?"

I nod lazily and twist the strands at the nape of his neck in my fingers absentmindedly. "Looks like. My turn now."

He laughs and leans his forehead against mine. "I'll let you have a taste, sweetheart, but I'm not coming in your pretty little mouth."

I pout at him, not happy with that thought. "And why

not?"

His hand runs along my side and dips into my crease. The calloused pad of one finger caresses my rim and I shiver at the touch. He licks his lips before leaning close to my ear and whispering. "Because I'm not coming until I'm deep in this little hole of yours."

Dear god, the man's trying to kill me with words. I'm going to die a virgin if he keeps this up. I tighten my fingers in his hair and pull his head back so our eyes meet again. "Is that so?"

I release his hair and drop my hands from his neck to press against his chest, giving him a shove and rolling him onto his back with me on top. "Then I better get my taste while I can, hmm?"

He spreads his legs, and I drop to my knees between them. "Taste whatever parts of me you'd like."

I tweak both his nipples, making him groan with a tug at them. "Even here?"

"Whatever you'd like."

I lean down and explore his chest with kisses and licks, followed by my hands, much like he'd done with me. I follow the marked lines of his abs, the faint lines of his six-pack visible enough for me to toy with. He sucks in a breath as I paint the lines with the tip of my tongue from bottom to top before I slide it all the way down his dark happy trail to the prize below.

His shaft is long with prominent veins, the girth of it hefty in my hand as I give it a solid stroke from base to tip. He groans and hisses yes, as if to encourage my exploration. With the flat of my tongue, I trace the most prominent vein from balls to tip before taking the cut head into my mouth for a hard suck. I may not know what I'm doing, but I'll for damn sure figure it out.

I lick and suck at him, stroking all the while. His moans spur me onward and I try to take him to the back of my throat like he'd done me, only to gag on it. He runs his fingers through my messy hair. "As sexy as that is, baby, don't push past what's comfortable for you."

Gah, even in the throes of lust and what I'm hoping is a damn good blow job, he's still looking after me. My heart warms in my chest and I renew my efforts. I drop my mouth down to take one of his balls inside and give it a suckle. I've seen it in the porn I've watched, so of course I had to try it.

As I release his ball to attack the other, I find myself flipped onto my back with a dazed-looking Rhodes hovering over me, his breathing ragged. "Had to stop you. Want to keep my promise."

His hand takes hold of my cock, already stiffening back up from tasting him as thoroughly as I'd done, even if I wish I'd been able to swallow him down like he had me. I moan at the contact as he leans in for a kiss, our tongues tangling together as he strokes me between us, heightening my lust all over again.

My hole twitches in anticipation of what's to come. I'm *so* ready for that.

Chapter 22
RHODES

He's a quick study. My sudden urge to come into his hot mouth nearly caught me off guard, almost ending our precious night all too soon. I take the time to stroke him as I battle myself back from the edge he'd taken me to.

Breaking the kiss, I sit up on my knees and motion to him. "Roll over onto your hands and knees."

He gives me a curious look before swinging his leg around and flipping over as I requested. He gazes back at me over his shoulder and arches his back, pushing his sexy, round ass in my direction. I groan at the sight. The man's just fucking beautiful as hell.

I curl my hands around his cheeks and stroke the soft flesh, splitting his cheeks and getting my first look at his hole. The urge to shove deep is there, but I hold back and lean in, letting my tongue tease at the furled skin, drawing a shout from Trevor. "Oh fuck, you're going to rim me?"

The husky chuckle I release is low and throaty as I nip at the skin around his hole. "You're damn right I am. Gotta get you ready to take me."

I run the pad of my thumb through the wetness left by my tongue. "I need to know how much prep you want. You said you're a virgin earlier, and I didn't question this then. Have you ever had anything in here, sweetheart?"

He blinks at me over his shoulder. "Oh my *god*, we're going to have this conversation *now*?!"

His tone holds exasperation, and I press against his hole, feeling him instinctively clench against the threat of intrusion. I go back to the soft caresses as I meet his gaze. "Give me an answer and I'll go back to getting you ready."

He groans and drops his head, as if unable to look at me while answering. "*Fiiinnnneeee*. I regularly use dildos on myself, about the size of you, cause I'm a size queen."

He looks back at me. "Happy now?"

I lean in and go back to licking along his entrance. "Fucking ecstatic."

He groans at my ministrations, and I take my time, licking and sucking at his rim before working my tongue inside, softening him up for my fingers to join into the play.

"Sweetheart? Reach into that drawer on the right and grab the lube and a condom."

He groans as I stab my tongue back in him and he stretches out for the drawer to grab out the supplies I'd forgotten to grab in my haste to get my hands on him. The man nearly makes me forget everything.

He tosses them onto the bed at his hips and I grab the

lube. With a soft snick of the cap, I coat my fingers and work him open, starting with one finger and then adding another. Trevor eases under my touch, relaxing to let me easily slip them inside. I work at stretching his rim as I lean down, placing kisses along his spine to his shoulder blades. I feel for the spongy spot inside him and as I caress that point, I whisper to him. "You ready for this?"

He shudders hard and gasps out, "Fuck yeah, give it to me, Rhodes, please!"

I slide a third finger within him and stretch him a bit more, not wanting to cause him any undue pain. After sitting up, I nab the foil packet with my free hand and rip it open with my teeth. I pull my fingers from within him and slide the condom down my aching cock, covering the deep purple head. I get up on my knees behind him, my hand aiming the shaft to his entrance.

I almost pause to ask him again if he's ready, but he's already said he was, so I press forward to breach the ring of muscle. "Time to let me in, baby."

As he pushes out, my head slips in, his muscle stretching to accommodate my width. I groan at the way his hole fits snug around my shaft as I slowly work myself deeper inside him with slow and short strokes, pausing whenever he tenses up and moving as he relaxes. When my hips meet his ass, I sigh with relief and bend over him, propping myself up on my hands to kiss his sweaty nape. "God, you feel like perfection."

He moans and presses back against me, and I flex inside him, my cock ready and eager for the ride. "You feel so good, Rhodes. More. *Move.*"

I give an experimental thrust, dragging my dick along

his prostate and drawing a long moan from his throat. His body lax beneath me, I move within him, giving him all he wants, and then more. Our groans, moans, and grunts fill the air as I take him over and over, the bed rocking into the wall as my thrusts get harder and harder.

There's only one last thing that would make this perfect. I need to see his face. Life has no guarantee, and neither is a second round of sex. I slow and pull myself from within him. "*Oh no*, I'm so fucking closer."

I chuckle softly and lean up off him, tapping his hip. "I want to see you come. Flip over."

He scoots his legs up and rolls over, pulling his legs up to his chest and baring his beautiful hole to me once more, eager and willing to have me fill him up again. I take the invitation and lean over him, sliding back home. We both sigh with relief and I lean down to kiss him as I resume thrusting hard.

I break the kiss to take hold of his shaft, stroking it to the tempo of my hips and he shudders hard and cries out, "Oh god, gonna come."

"Come for me, sweetheart."

With another cry of my name, his cock spurts, shooting white streams over my hand and our stomachs. Feeling his hole clench around me, I groan low and release inside him, jet after jet filling the condom separating us.

I hold myself over him, faces close and breathing harsh between us. I peck him before easing myself out of him. Tying off the condom, I toss it into the bedside trash before wiping my hand on a towel I'd left beside the bed. I pull it back with me and mop up his spend from the two of us. He hums, his eyes closed shut with a look of utter bliss on his face.

I toss the towel over my shoulder and wrap my arms around him, pulling him into my chest. He nuzzles into me with the sweetest of sighs. "Didn't know it could be like that."

I want to tell him it's never been like that for me, but I hold back, not wanting to scare him off before we decide anything. I kiss his forehead instead. "It was all I'd hoped it would be and more."

He laughs softly and opens those doe brown eyes to peer up at me. "Yeah?"

I nod. "Yeah. It was amazing."

He beams up at me and hugs me tight. Here in this moment, everything feels so right in my world, like it's all there for me to grasp. "So, how about we clean off in the shower and go watch for those stars for a bit?"

He chuckles and shakes his head. "You and those stars. You might have to carry me. Think you sexed out all my energy."

I can't help but laugh and do exactly as he asked, carrying him to the shower and then, after dressing us both, taking us out onto the deck.

Chapter 23
TREVOR

Oh. My. God. Why did no one tell me sex was *that* fucking amazing? Maybe it would've helped me get over myself enough to get out of my comfort zone earlier, but who knows? Maybe this was just my time. I couldn't have asked for a better man to lose my v-card to.

Rhodes is the complete package from what I've seen of him this weekend. I'm leaning hard toward giving whatever this is building between us a solid chance when the weekend's over. What more can a boy ask for? The man takes care of me while supporting me to be stronger on my own two feet.

Not to mention strong as hell as he carries me outside and settles down on one of the lounge chairs with me on his lap. I may be small in stature, but I'm not exactly a lightweight.

I cuddle into his chest as my eyes adjust to the darkness. With my head resting on his shoulder, we stare up at the brilliance of the stars we're able to see this far out in the country. While I might not consider it a pure dark area because of the resort's lighting, it's a sight more than I get to see in the city.

With his arms wrapped around my middle, I feel like I'm cocooned in warmth and safety high among the tree branches. Does it get any better than this? I don't think so.

The thought of leaving all this tomorrow pains me. I didn't think I'd get this close to anyone, but definitely not this quickly. It's as if I already know him somehow, but that's impossible. I'd have remembered meeting him. He's too damn hot to forget.

"That one is Ursa Major, or the giant bear. Part of it forms the Big Dipper."

He lifts his hand to point to a cluster of stars overhead as his words rumble in my ear, sending delicious signals to all parts of my sated body. Want to talk about a heavenly body? This man definitely has one. "Is that your favorite one?"

I feel him shake his head. "No. Let me see if I can find it in the sky. Might not be visible right now."

While he studies the sky, I stare up at the twinkling balls of light, hoping for one to fall so that I might wish upon it. Wish with all my might that Rhodes and I have a future. I gasp as one does. "Did you see that?"

He chuckles and kisses my temple. "Sure did, sweetheart. The space weather app I sub to said it was a good night for it, too. Talk about a bonus to a great weekend, huh?"

I stare at that space of sky, waiting to see if another will fall, enamored by the sight. My good friend Star-Gazer talking about the meteor shower being impressive this month seeps from my memory, causing me to smile fondly.

If I'm going to give Rhodes and me an honest shot, perhaps it's time to say goodbye to the flirtation with my guildmate. Even knowing I'll have to tell him when I get home, I whisper to the air, "Until the stars shine again."

"And sunlight hides from our gaze."

I'd been expecting Rhodes to say something about the stars, pointing out his favorite constellation. I was *not* prepared to hear those words coming from the man behind me. Freezing, my breath catches before I sit up and spin around to look at him, wide-eyed. "What did you say?"

Surely, I heard him wrong. It's wishful thinking I heard my guildmate's return phrase from the man I just spent an entire weekend falling for, right? *Right?*

The whites of Rhodes' eyes beam up at me in the darkness, showing me he's just as shocked as I am. His voice is whisper soft as he says those words a second time, "And sunlight hides... from our gaze. Aravar?"

It's him. He's StarGazer. All weekend long, when I've thought he reminded me of my guildmate, it's because he's *actually* him. My voice abandons me as I open my mouth to respond, so I nod instead.

His hand cups my cheek, his voice filled with awe as he speaks again. "Right there in front of me this entire time. How did we not see it?"

Great sex, and not only with an amazing guy, but an amazing guy who also happens to be my online crush? This boy has *got* to be dreaming. That's the only explanation.

Eliot's words before I left hit me, and I want to facepalm so hard. Not a RomCom superstar, that's what I'd said. Now look at me? Okay, so I may not be a superstar, but this is some straight up RomCom stuff for sure. He's never going to let either of us live this down.

As the pad of Rhodes' thumb brushes the ridge of my cheek, it brings my focus back to the two of us and the question he'd asked. I shrug and shake my head. "No clue. Perhaps not sharing personal details, we didn't hit on the little hints we had."

I lift my hand and tick a few points off on my fingers. "We both love video games. I enjoy being a healer while you prefer the front row action of a melee fighter. You love watching the stars."

I motion toward the sky like, hello, exactly what we were doing, then continue. "The puzzle pieces were there. They just didn't click."

He leans in to kiss me, as if this news hasn't rocked him off his axis like it has me. In my state of shock, I don't kiss back, making him pull away with a frown on his gorgeous face. "Are you upset it's me?"

I roll my eyes with a heavy sigh. "Not exactly. Frustrated, maybe? Definitely shocked. Maybe a little upset?"

He looks away from me, letting his hand fall from my cheek to his side. I'm sure I've hurt his feelings, but when it comes down to it, it's nothing about him or who he is. I reach to take hold of his chin and bring his face back toward mine. "I'm not upset it's you. You are amazing, and even from only knowing you as StarGazer, I've always thought that. But... I'm not the same person as the guy you've talked to on the game."

He frowns and his head tilts to the side like a confused puppy. "How so?"

I release of his chin and wring my hands together. "No one can see me behind my computer screen, so I can be the guy I am in my head. Yet, you've seen the real me this weekend. I'm awkward as hell."

I don't bring up the fact I always feel like a 'fraidy-cat-coward most of the time. No sense in reminding him of all the ways I'm a failure at this thing called life. The mere thought of such things has me dropping my eyes to his chest.

Crickets and other insects fill the quiet between us as he takes in my words. I squirm a bit, but stop, realizing I'm still on his lap and he'll feel it. Each moment passing amps up my anxiousness, so I move to get off him. He grabs my hips to stop me, drawing my eyes back to his. "Do you want to know what I've seen?"

No. No, not really. I don't say those words aloud. I swallow and just nod, cause hell, his words can't be any worse than what's already going through my brain.

"Yes, I've seen the awkward man, but he's so freaking adorable. All it's done is make me fall for him more. I've also seen him trying so hard to change his life. He's braved a trip with a man he didn't know and stayed for the entire thing. You're stronger than you think you are."

I blink a few times before staring at him. He thinks I'm brave? Tears spring to my eyes, but I fight to hold them back. It shouldn't be such a surprise to me. He's only looked out for me all weekend, done what he thought was best for me and my mental state. Why should now be any different?

Chapter 24
RHODES

The dim light reflects the shine in his eyes as he fights back tears. I don't want to make him cry, but I need him to see what I do. All weekend, I've been fiercely protective of the man from first glance, and nothing has changed for me. All I want is what's best for him. That's it.

His voice quivers as he replies, "You really think that?"

I rub his hips and nod. "Of course I do, sweetheart. And knowing you're Aravar? That only makes what I've seen even better. I know both sides of you now."

He seems to ponder over my words, so I go on. "Would it make you feel better if I told you a secret of my own?"

"What about the rule of not sharing personal details?"

I laugh and shake my head. "Think that one went out the window already, don't you?"

"Okay, so what's your secret, then?"

I'm really hoping I don't shoot myself in the foot with what I'm about to say, but he looks like I have flayed him open and he needs something to equalize the unfair advantage I have.

"I own PlagueDoc."

As much as he plays my game, there's no doubt he knows the company who made it. The PlagueDoc Studios logo is on prominent display when the game first loads up.

He stares at me, more shock upon his beautiful face. It's more shock than I thought he'd show, to be truthful. Sure, I know the ins-and-outs of the game and said nothing to the guild, but surely that can't be too surprising. I can't be the only CEO who plays their own game out there in secrecy.

"You own the game we met playing? *King's Ransom* is *your* game?"

"I do. It's my baby."

He groans and flops his head forward onto my shoulder. "This isn't happening. Tell me this isn't happening."

I frown. What the hell is up with *this* reaction? I've got to be missing something. I kind of expected him to laugh and shove at me for not sharing secret tidbits I know from insider knowledge. He's acting as if it's a grievous act I've committed against him. "I don't understand."

He groans again and lifts his head to stare at me before shaking his head. "Of course you don't get it. You don't know."

I want to roll my eyes at his reaction or shake him or something to get the answer out of him. "Don't know what?"

He looks up at the stars before looking back at me. "I've gone and fucked my boss."

At first, I'm confused. I'm pretty sure he told me before we had sex that he was a virgin, so how could he... Ooh. Wait, what? "You work for Plague?"

He nods his head miserably. "Yep. I'm one of the community moderators."

From his reaction, I was expecting him to tell me he was one of the developers, or, god forbid, a team manager of some sort. I let out a tiny sigh of relief at his words. While I don't have a rule against fraternization between work colleagues, it would look like poor form if I was in a relationship with one of the developers I'm directly responsible for.

"That's not that bad."

He lifts his head at me, all aghast. "How's it *'not that bad'*?"

He mimics my tone, doing air quotes along with the words. I can't help chuckling at his reactions. He's sometimes the most adorable little drama queen ever. "Because I'm not over the community teams. Yeah, I'm head of the company, but I've little interaction with that side of things. As long as things are on the up-and-up and fans aren't complaining, I consider it taken care of. I handle the developers and any fires that crop up in the business."

He looks confused at my words. "But the manager over us always says you know what we're up to."

I chuckle softly. "Well, yeah, they do report to me about community activities and such, but I don't manage that part. I've got an amazing VP who heads those efforts. If I had to deal with development and community management, I think I'd have lost my mind a long time ago."

He studies me for a moment. "So, if I logged into work tomorrow and told everyone what a horrible lay you are, you wouldn't know about it?"

"Horrible lay, my ass."

He snorts and pokes me in the side. "Yeah, yeah, you were awesome. Not the point. Answer the question."

"I might hear someone was saying rumors about me, but at most, you'd be a statistic that crosses my desk on the HR report."

He hums softly and toys with the hem of my shirt. "So, if we started something, it wouldn't cause problems?"

I shake my head and lean in to kiss his forehead. Just can't seem to keep from touching or kissing him, and I don't see a single problem with that. "Not at all. I'd give HR and my VP the heads up, just to keep everything all legitimate, but other than that, things would continue as they always have. No special treatment just cause you're dating the CEO."

He shakes his head. "I wouldn't want special treatment, anyway."

"Good. How about we go grab some sleep? I don't know about you, but my flight leaves out pretty early."

Trevor nods, yawning as the day catches up to him. Guess the shock of the night kept him up far later than it would've if all we'd done was star gaze. "Yeah, sleep sounds good."

I stand, pulling him up into my arms. Not expecting the sudden move, he squeals like a mouse and scrabbles for my shoulders. "Geez, Rhodes. A little warning next time?"

I laugh and wink at him. "Now, where's the fun in that?"

He rolls his eyes at me and rests his head on my

shoulder as I carry him inside and tuck him into my bed. I consider stripping off my lounge pants, but I'm not sure if sleeping in the nude will weird him out, so I leave them in place and climb into the bed behind him. Pulling his back into my chest, I wrap my arms around his waist and bury my face in the nape of his neck, placing a kiss upon the soft flesh. "I've got one last little secret."

Another yawn sounds from him as he nestles back into me as if he does it all the time. I can't wait to hear his answer in the morning on if he'll like all this to continue. Fingers crossed, he does. "What's that?"

Here goes that last little major tidbit I've been hiding all weekend. "I don't know if you've put the pieces together yet or not, but I should tell you my family owns Williamson Holdings."

Chapter 25
TREVOR

I freeze at his words. Williamson Holdings? I might've been a foster kid and raised poor, but even I'd heard of the Williamson family. Like Midas, it seems everything those people touch turns to gold and they're about as famous as the Kennedys.

No wonder *King's Ransom* and PlagueDoc have done so well. He's got *'the touch'*. Those aren't my words, a journalist said them once in an article I'd read years ago. With the backing of a family like that, how could he *not* succeed?

"Trevor? You okay?"

I squeeze my eyes shut and force my body to relax back into him. No doubt he felt me tense up. I take in a deep breath and lie my ass off. "Oh, yeah. Fine. I guess I just didn't connect those dots, either."

Connect those dots. Insert inner snort here. I'm hoping he doesn't call me on it. "You sure?"

I nod. What else can I say at this point? "Yeah. Let's

just sleep. We can talk more in the morning."

"Okay. Good night."

"Good night, Rhodes."

He nuzzles my neck again, and soon, his soft snores fill my ear. I lay there for a while, letting my thoughts race before forcing my eyes shut and attempt to sleep.

Fuck. My. Life.

❤·❤·❤

Sleep never came. I laid awake the rest of the night after Rhodes fell asleep. He'd started out the night holding on to me as if he couldn't believe I was in his arms. I can't blame him for that. It's hard for me to believe, too. What are the freaking odds that my mystery date and my online crush would be one and the same?

That I can handle no problem. I think it's awesome, but the rest? I'm in bed with the guy who's essentially my boss, my very rich and influential boss. Fuck my life. Yeah, I cursed, *again*. Sue me, but this is a situation that deserves a curse word. Probably several of them.

He's not just Rhodes. He's James Rhodes Williamson, the third, of the Williamson Holdings family, *and* owner of PlagueDoc Studios. He's not just my boss. He's big money and has a big name. What in the world would a man like that see in me for a long-term future? It's just ludicrous. I see only one way for our journey to go from here.

As the light of dawn peeks around the edges of the curtains, I ease from the bed, glad Rhodes had released me during the night to roll over so I'm not having to escape his hold. As I gather up my clothes and sneak from the room, I know I'm a giant coward. I can't face him and tell him I know I'm not good enough for him or his elite family.

I quickly gather all my belongings and toss my bags over my shoulders. Stopping in the kitchen, I grab the little memo pad on the counter and scratch out a quick note. While I'm a coward, I'm not heartless. I won't leave him hanging without a word. Leaving the note propped against the coffeepot, I go back to take one last peek into his bedroom. I take in his sleep-tousled hair and sleek muscles over the top of the blanket.

Tears burn my eyes, but I hold them back. If I sob now, he'll wake up and I just… I just can't tell him goodbye. I turn and make my way from the treehouse, all while praying he stays asleep so I'm able to make my escape from the resort completely without him running after me.

With quick steps, I make my way into the lodge to drop off my keycard and summon a ride to the airport. I pace the front porch while I wait, keeping an eye and ear out on the doors should Rhodes appear.

Luck seems to be on my side this morning. My rideshare pulls up to the lodge and I flop into the back of the car with my bags. As the driver heads down the tree-lined drive for the last time, I let the tears finally fall.

Chapter 26
RHODES

Beep, beep, beep. My alarm pulls me from a deep sleep, and I reach out to grab my phone off the nightstand and swipe across the screen to turn it off. I roll over to wrap my arms around a sleeping man but stop short, finding nothing but rumpled sheets. I was hoping for morning cuddles before we had to leave, but seems Trevor woke up before me.

A bit disappointed, I climb from bed and throw on a clean pair of lounge pants before heading out into the cabin while calling out. "Trevor?"

I go into the bathroom to handle my morning business, but as I finish up, I realize naught but silence greeted me when I called out Trevor's name. With a frown, I call again. "Trevor? Where are you?"

I peek into his room and see the bed undisturbed, but something seems off. *Where's his stuff?* I head into the kitchen to start the coffee. Surely if he had had such an early flight, he would've said something. We were supposed to talk this morning about whether we were going to continue after this weekend or not.

As I reach for the coffeepot, I spy the note waiting for me. I abandon my mission and pick up the scrap of paper to read it.

> Rhodes,
>
> I know we said we'd talk this morning, but I'm too much of a coward to do this face-to-face. While you're an amazing man anyone would be lucky to have, and much as I'd love for that man to be me, I know I'm not good enough for you. You'll say that I am, and I'm sure you'll believe your own words, but the moment I screw things up for you, you'll resent my existence in your life. You've built something amazing, and it deserves every chance to thrive. It's just better for me to do that from behind the screen.
>
> Thank you for the great weekend. I'll never forget it or you.
>
> Trevor

Chills roll over my skin as his words sink in. He's left. Not just the cabin, but me, too. Without even a word. His words on the page seem like he thinks so highly of me, but to deny me the right to my choice in this? Apparently, he doesn't think that much of me, despite his written words.

As shock gives way to anger, I crumble the note in my hand and growl. I pause as I go to throw the paper away. Might want to hold on to this. I know how to find him now. He works for my company and he's part of my guild. It'd be too easy to go crawling back to him on my knees to beg him for a chance. Perhaps I'm too proud, but I refuse to do that. None of this morning is my fault.

I set the wadded paper on the counter and smooth it out before folding it into quarters. I take it back to my room and slip it into my wallet. In weak moments, I can pull that out and re-read his words, reaffirm my commitment to staying away from him.

Even this cabin is tainted now. I pack my things up, cursing silly men all the while. Once done, I head for the lodge. I'll hang out there until it's time to head to the airport. Maybe I'll get some work done before I fly home.

♥·♥·♥

The silence is deafening. I drop my bag to the floor and the thud it makes against the hardwood echoes around me like a gunshot. My home has never felt as unwelcoming as it does at this moment. After the time spent with Trevor at the cabin, I'm not sure when my home will feel inviting to me again.

The mere thought of him nearly sends me to my knees as my eyes land on my gaming computer through my study door. Normally, I'd get comfortable and pop into the game. But now? It sounds more painful than relaxing. What if Trevor's online? Can I even take seeing his avatar?

Sure, I could change guilds and block him from my friends' list to avoid him, but it wouldn't take away all the memories, all the conversations we've shared. They still take up residence in my mind.

I'm not even excited to go to work in the morning like I normally would be. *Shit*. Is my baby going to be ruined for me forever because I'd lost Trevor and it was how we truly first met?

The weekend had been so amazing. I'd been planning to remember it for the rest of my life. Now? Now I just want to forget it ever happened. Go back to how things were, before I knew who Aravar was outside of the game.

Anger surges through me, so I make my way into my kitchen and open the rarely used cabinet over the fridge. I snag the bottle of whiskey I keep there, and spin open the top. Not even bothering with a glass, I take a healthy swig of the liquid, feeling the burn as it surges down my throat to warm my belly.

Fuck all this shit. It'd been torturing me all day and all I want to do is sleep until it's a faded memory. I down the rest of the whiskey, about a fourth of the bottle, in rapid succession. It's not enough to make me black out, but the edges of my vision go fuzzy.

Still wearing the clothes I'd flown home in, I face plant my bed and force myself to sleep. Thank fuck for alcohol.

Chapter 27
TREVOR

2 Weeks Later

> Dude, where the fuck are you?
> Eliot

I wince at Eliot's text and toss my phone back onto the bedside table with a clatter. I'd been avoiding the game like the plague since I got home, and dodging his text messages as well. He'd want the entire story of what went down and I'm just not ready to tell him. Like I'd told Rhodes, I'm just one big freaking coward.

My phone buzzes again and I ignore it. No doubt Eliot sent a follow-up message. I'll have to reply to him soon. Hopefully, by then I'll have some idea of what to say to avoid questions.

I glance around the hotel room. It's not as homey as the cabin had been. Just a standard room from your run-of-the-mill chain hotel with a single bed, nightstand, table, chest of drawers, and a TV. It's playing a random news channel for background noise as I get up to pace the room.

Work had sent me to Nerd Con to work at our booth. I'd been looking forward to it. Free tickets? Sign me up. I could explore when it wasn't my turn in the booth. While I'm still kind of glad for that, I'm really, *really* hoping that Rhodes isn't here. I've never worked the company events before, so I'm not sure if he even comes to these things. I could ask my boss, but I'm too much of a chicken crap to ask.

Yep, really brave man, right here. Everyone, come take a look.

As my phone buzzes again, moving along the surface of the table, I know I've got to look at it. This is a work function, and it could be my boss. I walk over, grabbing the device, and slide down the notifications. Nope. Both from Eliot.

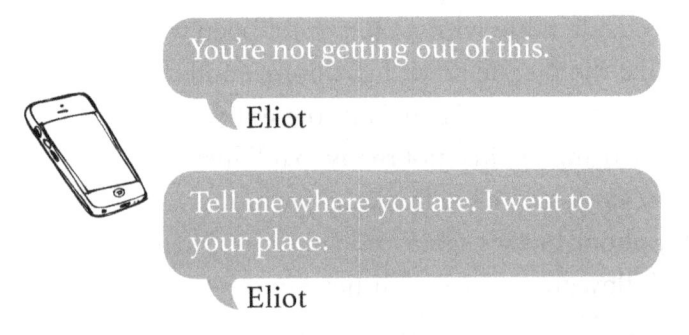

> You're not getting out of this.
> Eliot

> Tell me where you are. I went to your place.
> Eliot

Ah hell, of course he went by my apartment. The man's only my bestest friend in the entire world and I've never ignored him like this. I sigh heavily and type out a response. Can't leave him hanging anymore.

> I really don't want to talk about it right now. I'm at Nerd Con working the booth this weekend. Maybe when I get back home, we'll talk, but not this weekend. Pls?
>
> — Trevor

I sink down on the edge of the bed, staring down at the screen until his reply pops up.

> I'm holding you to that. Enough of whatever bullshit this is. Got me?
>
> — Eliot

> Got you. See you when I get back.
>
> — Trevor

I shove my feet into my shoes and my phone into my pocket as I stand. I don't even wait for a reply. Time for my first shift at the booth.

❤·❤·❤

My shift kept me busy the entire time and my mind off the wreck that's my life. I helped the developers and game artists wherever they needed me. It was neat meeting some of the people I'd interacted with on the forums over the last year, too. I'd not been expecting anyone to know me, but it's still cool to be recognized.

One of the developers, Michael, and I struck up a friendly accord. I'd spent most of my shift working next to him and learning a lot more about the game and its mechanics than I'd known from my work as a moderator. Talking to him fuels my want to go back to school and get a degree in game engineering.

I'd heard Rhodes hadn't come to this one. While I was glad I don't have to face him, I find myself oddly disappointed by his absence. I miss him like crazy, both as himself and as StarGazer. My life had never seemed as lonely as it had since I'd been avoiding the game and him. I'm going to have to face him in the future.

I look over at Michael as the two of us pack up backpacks and head from the booth. "Think I'm going to walk around and hang out for a bit. You game?"

He shakes his head with a radiant smile. "Nah, not today, man. I brought my girl along on this trip and it's our anniversary, so I've got a special night planned."

My heart pangs with a shot of longing, and I force a smile to my face. "That's cool. Congrats on the anniversary."

He thanks me and leaves, leaving me to the busy crowd all on my lonesome. Story of my life. Always alone, but it's in this moment I realize I've done it to myself. To keep myself safe from harm, I've done everything I could to keep people at arm's length. How Eliot slipped by years ago stumps me, but perhaps it's because he'd been in my last foster home as we'd both aged out close together.

I pull out the program for the convention and flip through it, seeing what events are going on. The words *Heroic Helmets* catch my eye and I notice the cast is doing a signing. Perhaps a picture of the cast will make Eliot happy with me after I've been avoiding him for so long.

I note where it's occurring and make my way to the area. The line is huge, and I head up to one of the staff keeping the line orderly. The guy gives me a stern look as he speaks. "You'll need to go to the back of the line for an autograph, sir."

Shaking my head, I pull out my phone. "I was wondering if I could walk right over there and take a shot of the table with the cast? I won't skip the line. Just want a photo."

I point to an area off to the right of the table out of the way of the crowd, but still has a good angle for a picture of the entire cast. The staffer looks at me with a dubious expression. "Just the picture. I won't hesitate to call security if you try to break the line."

I nod to the guy in thanks and leave him to his work in peace. I get into the place I'd pointed at and aim my phone. After the phone clicks, I pull up the photo to make sure it's a good one. A loud barked *'hey'* grabs my attention and my head jerks up to stare at this blond guy in front of one of the cast members.

I watch, along with a lot of other spectators, as the guy goes off on him. Part of his words really catch my attention. "My date donated his money to get you here. Is this how you treat your fans? He spent his hard-earned money, but isn't worthy of, like, five seconds of your time?!"

I frown, his words sinking deep into my soul as I realize what I'm watching. He's fighting for the man beside him. God, how I want someone like that, someone who'll defend me to the ends of the Earth and back again.

Rhodes rises to mind and tears spring to my eyes. Oh god, I'd *had* that. I'd thrown *that* away. Like a stupid idiot, I'd taken Rhodes affection and not just trashed it, I'd thrown it into a pit of lava after spitting on it.

I turn from the scene and rush from the room, not even bothering to thank the guy who'd let me get the picture. I fight back the tears all the way up the elevator and back to my room. *Dear god, what have I done?*

Chapter 28
RHODES

Anger doesn't even describe the mood I've been in the past couple of weeks. I think I've bounced around so many emotions most of my staff avoided me like the plague. I felt bad about that and have been trying to avoid dealing with people, letting Regina handle most things, but it's not so easy when my staff is so used to that personal connection.

This weekend is Nerd Con, so the office itself is blissfully quiet with few employees to bother. Originally, I'd planned to go, but when I saw Trevor's name on the list of attendees, I'd decided at the last minute to stay home, claiming a family emergency. My assistant didn't believe me, but she didn't push. No doubt she didn't want me biting her head off.

Instead of seeing all the fans of my beloved game this weekend, I've thrown myself headlong into work, much like I'd done since I'd come back from my vacation. Regina hadn't understood why someone would come back from a trip all riled up like I had, but I didn't bother to explain it to her, didn't want to admit someone found me wanting.

I hit save on the document I've been toiling on all afternoon as my cell phone rings. Seeing Dean's name, I cringe. He'd been trying to reach me since I got back, but I'd pushed him off, telling him I needed to get caught up from being gone. He'd called bullshit on me, claiming a weekend isn't long enough for me to get that far behind. Not like he's wrong, but I'm not admitting that either.

I silence the call and pull up the sprint logs for the week. I knew the team had been preparing for the trip, so there's not likely to be a lot on the spreadsheet, but I still wanted to go over the data.

I'm not sure how long I'm reading the screen when someone clears their throat in my open doorway. I glance up, ready to tell someone I'm busy, only to find Dean standing in the doorway.

"Guess the only way to get your attention is to show up at your office, hmm?"

I turn back to my screen and open a new document to begin typing up some notes I want to remember for the team based on the data I'd been reading. "I've had a lot to do."

The laptop's screen slams closed before my eyes and I jump, my eyes darting up to the angry hazel eyes of my best friend. "And it can wait till fucking Monday. Fuck, Rhodes. What happened to you, man?"

I frown at him. "What do you mean? You know I always work like the devil is hounding me."

His scoff is worthy of an Oscar. "Give me a break,

Rhodes. You went on that date weekend my friend Hudson worked hard on and I've not heard a word from you since. Not only have you dodged my calls, but now that I've seen you? You've lost weight."

I look down at myself, noting my clothes *are* baggy. Not enough for most to notice, but Dean knows me well enough to tell. I sigh and look back up at him. "Been too busy to eat?"

He rolls his eyes and sinks into the chair across from my desk. "Good thing I've got food being delivered. You talk while we wait. I ordered your favorite."

I sigh and sit back. I knew the minute I saw him, he would not let me push him off as easily as I had over the phone and text messages.

"Talk about what?"

My best friend rolls his eyes, reminding me of all the times Trevor had. Ugh. Is everything going to remind me of the man? Christ on a cracker, I need help. With another sigh, I start. "Fine. The weekend was amazing. I really liked the guy."

"If it was amazing, why the avoidance?"

Yeah, I'd not given him enough to connect the dots yet. Most people trip all over their feet when they discover who I am. The fact Trevor ran off? Rarely factors into the equation. "The night before we left, we'd been star gazing, and it came out we knew each other from before the weekend. The guy turned out to be the one I've talked about from my guild. You know the one."

Dean lets out a bark of laughter. "That's a heck of a twist. Still not finding the problem."

I scowl at him. "Before we fell asleep, I told him who

my family is. The next morning, he's gone with nothing but a note telling me anything we had was over."

Dean winces. "That had to hurt. I'm sorry, man. At least you know he didn't stay with you for the money."

I roll my eyes this time. "Yeah, like that's a comfort in my lonely bed at night."

A knock comes at the door and one of the security officers comes in, bearing the food. Chinese spices waft to my nose and my stomach growls loud in the quiet room. Both men stare at me and I shrug. "Guess I'm hungrier than I thought?"

Dean chuckles and takes the food from the officer, and he leaves us to our dinner. We sit quietly, stuffing food into our faces until Dean asks a question I'm not prepared for.

"If he came back, would you forgive him?"

Chapter 29
TREVOR

After a good long cryfest, I pace my hotel room. No, this can't be the end of our story. If I want a man who'll fight for me, I've got to prove myself worthy of fighting for. How the hell do I fix what I tore to shreds? Scotch tape won't help in this situation.

I bite on my thumbnail as I search my brain for ideas, yet nothing surfaces. I groan in frustration and stalk over to the table where my dinner grows cold and snatch up my phone, pushing the one contact I know who'll be there for me. Relief floods me as Eliot answers the phone. "It's about time, asshole. Home already? I thought you're supposed to come back on Monday."

"I do. I need your help."

No doubt he hears the plea in my voice as he instantly responds, "Just tell me where to bury the body."

I sink into the seat before the open window and stare outside. "No body. I screwed up something bad and I need help coming up with a plan."

"What'd you screw up?"

"Promise you won't judge me?"

He mutters something on the other end I don't catch. "You know I won't."

I sigh heavily. "Okay, so I'll tell you the complete story when I get home, but this is the short of it. I went on the date and fell for him. He turned out to be StarGazer, and he told me he's super rich. And when I say super, I mean mega *super* ultra rich."

I take a breath. "I freaked out and while he was sleeping, I left him a note and left."

Silence. I go back to biting my nail while I wait for Eliot to say something, anything. After what feels like forever, my best friend's voice fills the line. "Did you lose your v-card at least?"

I smack my head and growl a bit. "Oh my god, Eliot! That's not important right now."

"Of course it is. It's why you did all this, yeah?"

I roll my eyes. "Only part of it. You know I'm not a hook-up kind of guy. I was hoping for more and you know it."

He sighs. "I know, but you've got trust issues. We both do. Forever might not be in our cards. You know that, right?"

If he was here in person, I think I might've smacked him for that. "But what if it could be? What if he's my forever?"

More silence. Eliot's slow reactions are going to kill me before the end of this conversation, and it won't matter if I've got a plan or not.

"So, when you said you fell for him... you meant in

love, right? Did he feel the same?"

I shrug before answering. "It seemed like it."

Tears sting my eyes once again. "He's never going to forgive me, Eliot."

"Pfft," Eliot sounds over the phone. "If he fell for you too, and if he got to know the real you, he'll forgive you. Might have to work hard for it though."

I ball up my fist and take a deep breath. "I *knooow* that. That's why I need help. I need to come up with a way to talk to him. I checked the game, and he's not logged in since before the trip."

"So, you and StarGazer, after all. Fitting. Okay, so plan. If he's not logging into the game, you got his phone number?"

I shake my head. Yeah, I could message him through the Carousel app like I could've done prior to the trip, but that seems impersonal to me. I know I need to go big or go home here. "Nope. I know where he works…"

I trail off and Eliot pipes up. "What? You think of something."

"Yeah, just… okay, you've got to swear you'll keep this secret. I shouldn't be telling you, but I'm in dire need of help here."

"I would never break your trust. I swear."

I nod. "Okay, so he owns PlagueDoc."

The gasp is loud in my ear. "No way, really? The secrets he knows and hasn't shared. Tsk tsk."

Eliot's reaction draws a relieved laugh from me. "Yeah, said the same thing to him when I found out."

"Okay, I won't say anything, but what's that got to do with anything?"

"Well, I made friends with one of the developers today. What if I can convince him to make a private quest and we somehow get Rhodes to go on it? I'll be the reward waiting at the end."

Eliot hums. "Don't see how that's going to get him to forgive you."

I chuckle softly and put the phone on speaker to pull up my notes app on my phone. "By itself, no, but it might just get me in the door."

♥·♥·♥

I rush to the booth the next morning, hoping and praying. When I spy Michael in his seat at the table, I cheer inwardly. So far, so good. Now, to convince him of my plan. I sink into the chair next to him and give him a warm smile. "Morning, Michael. Have a good night?"

The man laughs, but his eyes light up at the mention of his girl. "Oh, hell yeah. I didn't say this yesterday since I didn't want to jinx myself, but I proposed to her, and she said yes."

I'm glad for the guy, really I am, but I'm doubly glad for me. Maybe he'll understand what I'm trying to do and get on board with helping me. It's worth a shot. "That's awesome! Congrats!"

"Thanks. Hope you'll come to the wedding whenever we decide to have it."

I laugh and nod. "Oh yeah, I'll be there. Count me in."

I bite my bottom lip and check the time on my phone. The con doesn't open for another hour, so I've got time on my side to convince him to help me. "Would that news put you in a good enough mood to help a new friend fix a relationship?"

Michael raises a brow at me. "Oh? Do tell."

Glancing around us, I make sure no one's listening in and lean close. I whisper my tale of woe, being sure to keep Rhodes' family out of it. Just saying that I freaked out over something big and ran out without talking to him. Michael whistles and stares me down. "I don't know how I'll be able to help with that."

"It's the idea I have. Should probably tell you that the guy is Rhodes."

Michael gapes at me. "Oh hell, you're the reason, aren't you?"

My eyes wrinkle in the corners as I frown at him, totally confused. "Reason for what?"

"Why Rhodes has been on a warpath for the last two weeks. Damn man, you've got him seriously in a mood that won't quit."

The words make me feel worse than I already do about what I did, but they give me hope. If he's still mad about it, there's a chance the weekend meant as much to him as it did to me. "That bad?"

Michael's nod is huge as his head bobs widely up and down. "Oh yeah. Rhodes is usually an easy-going guy and none of us have ever seen him this mad, even when the worst bug ever got unleashed into the world and none of us caught it."

I wince. I know what bug he's talking about. Somehow, a new quest got released to the game, which hadn't gone through quality control. Every time a player talked to the quest giver, it crashed the server. I'd just started as a new moderator right before it happened. The entire episode almost made me quit. "Oh yeah, that was bad. I'm sorry I've caused everyone so much trouble. If this works, it'll put a smile back on his face."

I try to end my words with a cheerful statement. I really need his help. Otherwise, I'm not sure what I'll do other than crawl to Rhodes on my hands and knees and beg for my life.

Michael studies me. "How can I help?"

I grin and lean in to share my idea. Fingers crossed, this is going to be *epic*.

Chapter 30
RHODES

Would you forgive him?

The question still echoes in my mind a week later, and I still don't have an answer. The talk with Dean had gotten me to settle down at work at least. Things were easier, as I was in a thoughtful mood rather than an angry one.

Maybe it would help if I understood why he ran from me. It had tempted me to log into the game all week and force him to talk to me, but maybe I'm a bit of a coward, too. I don't want to get shot down twice. I might take risks sometimes, but this one, the risk to my heart, it's just too great to take that leap.

A knock on the door has me looking up to find my assistant peeking in at me. "Hey boss, got a min?"

I nod and sit back to give her my attention. "Sure. What's up?"

She steps into the room but doesn't sit down like she usually does. "Michael is on the line for you. Says he's got a special quest he wants you to see? I didn't know you'd commissioned a new one."

Confusion is clear on her face, and no doubt matches my own as I frown. "What quest? I haven't commissioned anything new since they got back. That meeting isn't until next week."

She motions to the phone. "Maybe you'll get more out of him than I did. He refused to answer my questions."

I nod. "I'll take care of it."

She leaves the room as I pick up the phone. "Michael?"

"Hey boss. Sorry to bother you, but while I was at Nerd Con, an idea for a new quest for Valentine's Day hit me. I've got a prototype waiting on your test server and I would love to hear your thoughts on if I should polish it up or not."

I glance at the calendar, wondering if I've missed some months or something. "But Valentine's isn't for a few months."

The developer laughs. "Yeah, I know. I got engaged last weekend and it kind of spurred the idea."

I swallow the sad little sigh wanting to slip from me. "I'll let you know when I've got time—"

"Today. Now. I'm really, *really* eager to get your feedback on it. The final quest format will need better writing, and I want to send it over to the content team ASAP. Then the graphics peeps. You know the drill."

Someone's being a demanding little shit today. "Fine. You're lucky it's a slow day for me or I wouldn't be doing this. Don't make it a habit."

"Won't happen again, Rhodes. Promise."

Something about the way he says those words makes me curious, but I shove it away and pull up my test server. "How long is it?"

"Shouldn't take more than thirty minutes. Maybe less if you're lucky."

"Alright. I'll call you back when I'm done."

"Um, sure thing. Later."

Michael hangs up before I can question the flippant way he'd responded to hearing from me, but my character loads and I turn my focus to the screen. I'm not surprised to see my work avatar standing before the quest giver already. The team usually saves me time by loading me into exactly where I need to be. I click on the toon with the gold exclamation mark over their head to start the quest, initializing the text dialogue.

'Oh, thank all the gods you're here. I need your help! Bandits kidnapped my partner. You must find them and bring them home to me. Please, I beg you!'

I click through to answer all the prompts until the quest pops up in my quest log and the name of the quest is like a dagger to my heart. The Sweetheart Quest. It's like the universe is out to get me. I sigh and look at my map for where I need to go and my character calls his mount.

I find myself drawn into the quest, even with how rudimentary it is. Michael's always been one of my best and even in this, it shows. I head down a myriad of caves, sometimes hitting dead ends and having to retrace my steps. I fight enemy after enemy in what seems like a hefty bandit camp.

My character finds his way into an enormous cavern

where the main boss waits for him. The fight is intense, and I enjoy every minute, throwing all my energy into defeating the massive brute and his cleric partner. Before long, the two are dead at my feet and I'm victorious.

I pump my fists in the air, preparing to congratulate my developer when I spy the large cell at the back of the cavern. The key I'd looted off the main boss must be for that. I walk over and activate the door, watching as it swings open, and I stop still. There in the cage is not some random character. It's Aravar.

I gasp and lean forward in my seat. How the hell did Michael know to put him there? Or are my eyes deceiving me? I push the keys to have my character move to interact with Aravar's, but no matter how many times I click on the character, it does nothing. Absolutely nothing. It's almost like Michael forgot to make him interactive.

I growl at the unmoving avatar on my screen. "Sure, put the man I want in front of me, and he won't even respond."

Someone clears their throat and a timid voice reaches my ears, a voice I'd missed with desperation. "He will if you're willing to listen to him."

My head whips toward my door to find Trevor not as a character in the game, but in the flesh, hovering in the doorway as if unsure of his welcome. Even with how mad I am, I've never seen a more beautiful face in my entire life. I stare at him, speechless.

He shuffles from foot-to-foot and looks down at the carpeted floor of my office. "Um, may I come in?"

His question draws me from my stupor, and I stand, honestly confused about how he got to be here. I nod and he steps in, shutting the door behind himself. "It's great to see you, Rhodes."

Anger wars with the confusion inside me, and I fold my arms over my chest. The man has a lot of gall to show up here unannounced like this. The social niceties abandon me. "What are you doing here?"

My words come out curt, and maybe even a little cold. His flinch is visible, as if he wants to recoil from my words and my presence. I ease my stance a bit, but don't apologize. He sighs and raises his gaze to meet mine. "Are you willing to listen to me?"

I fight the urge to roll my eyes at his stall. "You're in here, aren't you? If I wasn't, I would've told you to get out."

He nods and drops his head before forcing it back up to look at me. His shoulders straighten like he's preparing to go to war, and perhaps he is. I'm not making this encounter easy on him. "I'm sorry for leaving you like I did. After all you did to make me comfortable that weekend, I crapped all over it."

I nod. It's not like I can argue his point. Apologies, however, do me little good right now. "Why'd you run off like that?"

"I told you in the note. I'm a screw-up and you deserve better. For all your talk of how brave I am, I showed you just how much of a coward I really am."

"Why do you think you're such a screw-up, or that you'd screw things up for me? I don't get it."

He sighs and sits in the chair, putting him at a level below me, like he doesn't deserve to stand and face me. I don't like that, so I sit down as well, keeping the desk between us. "You saw how I reacted to you on that porch.

I'm like that with most new people. I... I have trust issues, I know that. You deserve a man who can stand proudly at your side, proclaiming how great you and your work is."

He bites his bottom lip, and his eyes turn shiny with unshed tears. "I'm scared I can't be the man you need."

I sigh and shake my head. "So, you gave up, not even wanting to try? I wasn't enough for you."

Those doe eyes widen, and he shakes his head. "That's not true! That's not true at all. You're the best man in the entire world. No one, ever, has made me feel as cherished and safe as you did that weekend. No one!"

I don't soften to his plight. Do I even have forgiveness within me?

Chapter 31
TREVOR

I'm too late, waited too long to come to beg for his forgiveness. Tension takes over his entire form, and the look on his face? It's heartbreaking. Some anger still shows within the blue depths of his eyes and it's killing me.

I drop my eyes to the floor. Everything within me is telling me to flee, to just run out that door and not look back. The old me would've done it, but I came here to grovel and win him back. I'll do that at damn near any cost.

I almost don't catch his question while caught up in my misery. "Why should I believe you now? What's changed?"

I dare to meet his gaze again, and the words rush out of me. "Me. *I've* changed. I saw a guy at Nerd Con fighting for his date's right to something at one of the panels. It made me want that. It was then I realized that you'd already given me that, shown it to me the entire weekend, and I threw it all away."

I look down as a few tears escape, trying to hide them from his unwavering stare. Taking a deep breath, I continue. "I knew before I ever came here, words wouldn't be enough. Heck, maybe even coming here won't be. But I knew I had to prove it to you. I'm willing to fight for us. I only hope I'm not too late."

The last part of my statement is so soft, I'm not sure he could hear it across the desk. Fear wraps its threads around my heart, wrenching it from side to side as if to rip it into pieces all over again.

His next words are almost as quiet as mine. "And if I ask you to leave?"

I dare to sneak a peek at him from beneath my lashes. The hope I'd carried with me through the door when he didn't immediately shut me out dashes to the ground at my feet, seeing that stern look still upon his gorgeous face. I swallow. "I'll come back. Again and again until you realize I'm in this for the long haul or… you tell me to never return, that you could never forgive me."

Holding my breath while waiting for his reaction, I drop my head to my chest. I'm almost sure I'm about to be escorted out by security, but there's this one tiny kernel of hope still within me he's not about to turn me away. I reach up to wipe away a new tear tracking down my face as a hand grasps hold of my chin and tilts my face up.

I never heard him move, never saw him walk around his desk, but he's there, standing before me, touching me again. My breath hitches, caught in my chest as I stare into his eyes, the icy anger beginning to leech from them. "And if you get scared again?"

"I'll run to you. Let you help me chase it away."

He studies my face, that gaze roving over my features as if looking for my honesty. I hold still and go on. "I know I'll get scared again, but I promise you, Rhodes, I won't run away from you again."

"And you're sure this is what you want? Me?"

"With every beat of my heart. I love you, Rhodes."

He closes his eyes and a tear drifts down his cheek. I hold my breath once more and wait. He whispers, "Come here, sweetheart."

He tugs me up from my seat and I throw my arms around his neck, his own arms wrapping tight around my body. It feels so fucking good, so fucking right, being held in his arms again. I never want to leave his side. He's stuck with me now.

My hair muffles his words, but they still reach me. "I love you so much, Trevor. Never do that again. I don't think I'd survive it."

He doesn't have to beg me twice. I know I wouldn't survive either. "No, I won't. I promise."

He pulls back from the tight hug we'd wrapped each other in, a smile crossing his face as he looks at me. "In this till the end?"

I laugh softly and smile my first genuine smile in weeks. "Not even the mob boss could tear me away."

He laughs before leaning down and taking my lips with his. I lean into the kiss, opening my mouth to let his tongue inside to explore. We lose ourselves in the kiss, tongues tangled and hands beginning to wander. I'd thought I'd lost his touch for good, that I'd never know this love again. I've never been so glad to be proved wrong in my entire life.

As our kiss ends, he leans his forehead against my own and breathes in deeply, like he's not taken a good breath in a long while. I only have one last question for him.

"So, how do you like your quest reward?"

Epilogue
TREVOR

3 Months Later

I move my second monitor into place next to the main one and stand back, purveying my new gaming space in Rhodes' house. Well, our house now. With a nod of my head, I consider it done and relax.

It's been a long day, us moving me into the house with him. He'd wanted me to move in when we made up, but even though we loved each other, it still felt too soon to me. Yeah, I knew him as StarGazer, but we'd only had that one weekend together.

I convinced him I needed dates, and proper ones at that. He needed to woo me. He'd laughed at my word choice, but woo me, he did. The man knows the way to my heart, and with each day, he shows it more and more.

I bite my bottom lip, thinking about the past three months I'd spent with Rhodes. Just like the trip weekend, he'd been there for me every step of the way, showing me in all the ways how much he loved and cared for me.

Am I enough for him, though? The old fear slithers through my mind and I stare unseeing at my gaming setup. What if he regrets moving me in? I could still…

Arms wrap around me from behind, and a deep rumble sounds in my ear. "I love you."

Those words chase the fear from my heart, and I spin in my boyfriend's arms, looking up into Rhodes' handsome face, his warm smile warming me up inside where I'd grown cold moments before. It's as if the man senses when I'm faltering and shows up to reassure me. There's hope one day I won't need such reassurance, but apparently, this is not that day.

I return his smile. "I love you, too."

I don't know why I'm still worried. He'd already taken me to meet his family. It was rocky at first, with me stumbling all over myself, trying to prove myself worthy of Rhodes. I was sure I'd made such a fool of myself, but his mom, bless her heart, has the same fierce protective streak as her son and she'd taken me under her wing, providing me a safety net to grow more comfortable in the rich surroundings. It's a work in progress.

Rhodes takes my mouth in a searing kiss, taking my breath away like he always does. I press against him as my cock hardens in mere moments of his tongue against my own. I moan into the kiss as his fingers clench my cheeks and he hauls me harder against his body, grinding his hips into mine in a dance as old as time.

He breaks from the kiss to drop to his knees, that blue gaze staring lovingly up at me. "How about we christen *our* gaming room?"

As he goes to unbutton my pants, my phone pings and vibrates in my pocket, making me groan as I pull it out and see a text message.

> Quit sexing up the BF. Raid in 10 mins.
> Eliot

I sigh and look back at my man. "No time. We promised the guild we'd be on time for the raid."

Rhodes lets out a groan, but then looks up at me with the most wicked grin on his face. "I can work with that."

Rhodes gets me out and into his hot mouth within seconds. I groan in pleasure at the feel of his hard pulls on my dick, losing myself to the feel of his mouth on me.

And wouldn't you know it? We made the raid on time... barely.

THE END

Acknowledgments

Thank you for reading The Sweetheart Quest.

To the readers who've been with me since the beginning, this book is for you guys. I appreciate the support more than you know. This book was a long time in coming.

To all the new readers, I'm glad to you picked up my book and hope you enjoyed the ride.

This book wouldn't exist with out my fellow authors who came together to put this series on for you all. Huge thanks to them and it was amazing to work with you all. Look forward to more in the future.

And lastly, to my best friend, Saffron. You kept me sane when I could've melted down over so much throughout the past few months. Thank you!

About the Author

I'm a dreamer, ever with my head in the clouds. Some of my earliest memories are getting in trouble at school while looking out the window, daydreaming instead of doing my work. Fast forward quite a few years (okay, a few decades) and I can still be found staring off into space with flights of whimsy and pictures in my head. (Just an FYI, I'm probably not staring at you. Lol.)

I'm a huge addict to the feeling of falling in love, which is clear by the fact I've been obsessed with romance novels of all varieties since I was around eleven years old. I've got a gigantic love for chocolate, sweet tea, and coffee. At any point in the day, I guarantee I have one of those in my hands without fail, or you'll find a very grumpy Jacy.

Married with two kiddos, I've made my home in Oklahoma, which makes for some great storm chasing (even if it's done digitally through my computer for now). When I'm not writing or reading so many great MM stories, you can find me usually doing something artistic. From designing things in Photoshop to crochet and DIY projects, I'm not a happy girl unless I'm doing something creative.

♥·♥·♥

Get up-to-date info by signing up for my newsletter, Jacy's Musings. (news.jacybraegan.com)

I've also got a reader's group, so come join in on the fun and updates! facebook.com/groups/jacysloveaddicts

Follow me on Social Media!

Facebook Page: facebook.com/jacybraeganwrites
Instagram: instagram.com/jacybraegan/
YouTube: youtube.com/@jacy-braegan
TikTok: tiktok.com/@jacybraegan

ALSO BY JACY BRAEGAN

Oklahoma Hearts

Catching Blue Jay (*Book 1*)
mybook.to/catching-blue-jay

Standalones

The Secrets of Love Letters
mybook.to/SecretsofLoveLetters

Made in the USA
Las Vegas, NV
29 January 2025